LOST & FOUND

Julia Blake

*To Sophie
Best wishes
Julia Blake x*

copyright ©Julia Blake 2017
All rights reserved

Sele Books
www.selebooks.com

This is a work of fiction. All characters and events in this publication, other than those in the public domain, are either a product of the author's imagination or are used in a fictitious manner. Any resemblance to actual persons, living or dead, or actual events is purely coincidental.

No part of this publication may be reproduced, distributed, or transmitted in any form or by any means, without the written permission of the author, except in the case of brief quotations embodied in critical reviews and certain other non-commercial uses permitted by copyright law.

For permission requests contact the author.

www.juliablakeauthor.co.uk

ISBN: 9781974628520

Lost & Found is written in British English and has an estimated UK cinema rating of 12+ containing mild violence, occasional bad language and mild sexual references

Lost & Found is an Authors Alike accredited book

~Dedication~

To my parents, as ever, thank you.

To all my family, friends, and readers
Thank you for your continuing support
and for believing in me

~ *Acknowledgements* ~

A big thank you, as ever to my wonderful editor Dani. Thanks, missy, you are a stern taskmaster, but I wouldn't have you any other way.

Thank you must also go to my eagle-eyed beta readers, Caroline Noe, and Trisha J. Kelly. Both talented authors, you can find them at:

carolinenoe.org
facebook.com/TrishajkellyAuthor/

Finally, a massive thank you to James and Becky Wright at Platform House Publishing for all their patient help with formatting and all their advice and creative input with the fabulous cover and interior graphics. Thanks, guys, you are amazing.

For all your publishing needs, contact Becky on:

www.platformhousepublishing.co.uk

~A Note for the Reader~

This book is a new departure for me, shorter, and more intense, it's a fast-paced, punchy, roller-coaster of a read, and I hope you will enjoy reading it as much as I enjoyed writing it.

This is the first in a seven-book series about the Blackwood Family, as I felt each wonderful family member deserved their own story to be told.

As always, you can contact me on:
Facebook: Julia Blake Author
Instagram: @juliablakeauthor

And you can read all about my crazy life on my weekly blog "A Little Bit of Blake" on

https://juliablakeauthor.home.blog

You can also find out all about me and my books on my website:

www.juliablakeauthor.co.uk

~ The Blackwood Family ~

ONE
Legend of a Man

THREE
Very Different Wives

SIX
Individual Children

SEVEN
Extraordinary Tales

This is...

*THE
BLACKWOOD
FAMILY SAGA*

~A Family History ~

The Blackwoods are a wonderful, eccentric, rambling family. To quote Luke Blackwood – "they might be a hotchpotch of exes, steps and halves, but they're my family and I love them."

Originally founded by George Blackwood, a legendary fighter of a man, he and his first wife Celeste built a business empire between them and had two children, Monica and Marcus. But pressure soon split the perfect family cleanly down the middle with Celeste returning to her native New York and taking Monica with her, Marcus remaining in Britain to be raised by his father to take over the business one day.

George then fell immediately into another marriage with Marina, and for a while, things looked to be going his way, especially with the rapid arrival of their two children Luke and Susannah. However, George was soon left heartbroken when this marriage also disintegrated, with Marina stating she would always love him but could no longer stand the pace of his life and of always coming second to his business. The pair remained firm friends, Marina even taking on the upbringing of George's eldest son, Marcus.

Alone and working too hard, the inevitable happened and George was hospitalised following a heart attack. Regaining consciousness after surgery, the first thing George saw, were the laughing green eyes of his Irish nurse, Siobhan.

Two months later the pair were married, and despite the thirty years age difference between them, were blissfully happy for ten years, during which time Siobhan bore him two children, a son called Liam and a daughter called Kristina (Kit).

The whole family were devastated though when George, by then in his late sixties, suffered another heart attack and died, leaving behind three women who had all loved him passionately in their own ways, six children and one granddaughter, Megan, the child of his eldest daughter, Monica.

He also left behind a sizeable legacy to be split evenly between them, a multi-million pound business empire now ably run by his eldest son, Marcus, and a deep-seated work ethic tempered by bone-deep integrity and a sense of morality.

So that's the state of affairs in the Blackwood family at the beginning of this series. None of the children are currently married, except for Monica, a real estate agent in New York. Marcus is a business tycoon and a much sought after social batchelor. Luke owns and runs ICRA – the International Child Recovery Agency. Susannah owns her quirky little bookshop. Liam is a war photographer, and Kit is an up and coming opera singer.

All are happy and settled in his or her life, and each has no idea of the adventures they are about to embark on.

Book 1 of the
Blackwood Family Saga

Julia Blake

~Chapter One~
"I don't have a daddy."

It happened so suddenly. One moment Lucia was there beside her, chattering about this and that, sticking her tongue out to catch the lashing rain, the next...

The next she was gone, lost, snatched away from her in a desperate crush of tourists. Frantically, Arianna spun around, her eyes scanning the crowd.

"Lucia!" she cried, panic clutching her heart. "Have you seen a little girl?" she begged the passers-by. "Seven years old in a pink raincoat, long dark hair in plaits."

Strangers shook their heads, their faces masks of sympathetic curiosity as she darted from one to another, fear for her lost child rendering her almost incomprehensible.

Finally, she stopped still, trying to calm her racing brain, trying to think, think, think. All the time her mother's soul remembering news headlines, fearing the worst...

"You're the best brother ever, Luke. Thank you so much, I owe you big time." With his sister's words still ringing in his ears, Luke Blackwood plastered what he hoped was a sincere smile of welcome onto his face and stepped forward to serve the first customer of the week, his first customer ever if the truth be known.

Twenty minutes later he slumped, exhausted, behind the till, realising it was going to be worse than he ever imagined.

"You'll be fine," Susannah had reassured him. "It's easy, I promise. All you do is guide people to the right shelves and then take their money. I mean, how hard can it be?"

Luke had the sneaking suspicion Susannah's tongue had been firmly in her cheek, and if the other customers were going to be as demanding, difficult, and downright awkward as the first one, it looked as if he was in for a long week.

He only had himself to blame. He *had* offered to mind the shop for Susannah whilst she went on a much-needed holiday, a holiday booked for months but at the last moment looked like being cancelled when her capable assistant was rushed into hospital with appendicitis.

Hell, what big brother could have seen the devastated disappointment in his kid sister's big, blue eyes, heard the quiver in her voice, and not have offered to help, especially knowing how fragile Susannah was following the meltdown of her marriage. So, he stepped up to the mark. After all, he was off work himself recovering from the disaster of his last assignment.

Pulling a wry face, Luke gingerly felt his tender side. It was recovering quicker than the doctors had thought possible but still ached. He knew too much physical exertion would simply pull the wound wide open again.

A frown marred his rugged, handsome face as he remembered that night a month ago. They had been tracking the target for days when he finally settled in an old farmhouse deep in the Tuscan countryside.

Luke and his colleague went in alone, not expecting any trouble. Info on the mark agreed he was a mild-mannered, quiet man, not the sort to play hero, just a normal guy driven to desperate measures.

For a moment Luke felt a twinge of sympathy for him, then remembering the desperate grief and fear on the face of his client back in England, firmed his resolve and went in, determined to end this job now and take the package home.

It went smoothly at first. The guy sitting at an old, rickety table in the kitchen looked up at their approach. Luke saw weary acceptance cross his face, then he nodded his head towards one of the closed doors.

"In there," was all he said.

Leaving his colleague to keep an eye on him, Luke quietly opened the door and found himself standing in a dimly lit room.

Looking around, he saw the huddled shape on the bed and gently moved closer, anxious not to panic its occupant.

"Who are you?" The voice was high, young, and female.

"My name's Luke," he replied, his voice calm and steady. "I've come to take you home, honey. Your mummy is missing you very much and I know she'll be so happy to see you."

"Mummy?"

There was movement, and the child sat up. Luke saw her clearly for the first time in the shaft of moonlight angling through the bare window.

"But he ... Daddy ... he said she was ill, too ill to look after me anymore."

Luke's heart twisted at her words, at her pale, little face, scared and anxious in the dim light. Her words were familiar. During his lengthy career running ICRA – the International Child Recovery Agency – they were words he heard many a child utter. Their worlds ripped apart by parents who couldn't part amicably, whose desperation had led to one of them taking drastic action – snatching their child and absconding with them.

"Your mummy's better now," was all he said, holding out a comforting hand to the frightened child. "Come on, I'm here to take you to her."

The child hesitated, and then something in Luke's steady gaze seemed to reassure her. She held out her hand and allowed him to lift her gently from the bed and carry her into the kitchen, where the man, her father, still sat.

"Daddy?" Luke heard the confusion and conflicting emotions in the child's voice.

"Jenny!" The sight of his small daughter being carried away from him, possibly forever, seemed to galvanise him out of his previous lethargy.

"No!" he shouted, jumping to his feet so violently that his chair crashed to the ground.

"No!" he shouted again, and it was then it happened. Taking Luke's colleague by surprise, he leapt towards Luke, who turned to keep the child away from her father's hungry grasp.

Suddenly, from nowhere it seemed, there was a knife in the desperate man's hand. There was no time for Luke, his arms full of screaming, kicking child, to do anything more than propel himself backwards.

So instead of the knife burying itself in his stomach, it plunged into his side, drenching

Luke in red hot pain which he thrust away from, even as his fist punched upwards to send the man spinning to the ground, unconscious.

Once again, Luke felt his side, the twinge of pain and the snap of annoyance at the enforced weeks of rest the injury had caused.

Of course, he'd still been going into the office to conduct interviews, clear paperwork, chase up leads and carry out research on the internet, but he employed staff to do all those things.

After a while, it became clear that whilst he was stomping around the office like a bear with a sore head, he was preventing them from getting on with their work. Work they could carry out more smoothly and efficiently without him.

Then Susannah called round, voice quavering with disappointment. Her much longed for, much needed, holiday was to be cancelled because her assistant was in the hospital, and there was no one to run her business.

Knowing how important her little shop was to her, knowing how much Susannah needed a break, Luke somehow found himself offering to look after it for her for a week.

After all, it was only a bookshop. As she said, how hard could it be?

Luke sighed, tapping his hand on the countertop. The fact that he rarely had time to read these days hadn't seemed a problem at the time. If he were honest, the only thing he could remember reading in the past five years was the instructions for his new stereo.

Now, after having spent the last twenty minutes having his total ignorance of literature brutally pointed out to him by an irate, elderly spinster in a flowery rain bonnet, he knew he would rather face a whole army of rampaging parents armed with steak knives.

He was right. It was going to be a long week.

"Hello."

Luke looked down at the bright voice which abruptly seemed to pop up out of nowhere. It was a little girl with long, dark curls contained in two plaits, tied with pink ribbons bedraggled from the rain currently lashing against the shop window.

He estimated her age to be about seven or eight. Her raincoat was pink, with brightly coloured flowers patterned all over.

Beneath were pink trousers and a matching sweater, the whole outfit finished off with pink wellies with fairies flying gaily all over them.

Luke blinked. In his experience, children this age usually came with a guardian of some description. He looked expectantly at the door, waiting for an adult to come bustling in after the child. No one came. He looked back at the girl and frowned.

"Hello," she said again.

"Hello," replied Luke. "Can I help you?"

"I expect so," said the girl, cheerfully. "My name's Lucia Santorini, and I've lost my mummy."

The name was Italian, yet the accent was as British as steak and kidney pie, and Luke blinked again, almost stupidly, at this pink and forthright pixie that had suddenly appeared from nowhere.

"Oh dear," he said slowly. "Do you think I should phone the police?"

"No," the girl child called Lucia said and held out a piece of folded paper to him.

"This is my mummy's mobile phone number. Please can you call her and tell her where I am?"

Luke took the paper, part of his mind registering his approval at the good thinking of the child's mother, whilst he drew out his mobile and dialled the number.

"Yes?"

The phone was answered almost before it rang, the voice female, breathless, and scared. Luke imagined the panicked searching of a mother looking for her lost child.

"Hello," he replied, reassuringly. "Your little girl just came into my shop."

"Oh, thank heavens!" came the gasped reply. "Thank you so much. Where are you?"

Quickly, Luke told her, put his mobile away, and handed Lucia her important scrap of paper.

"Thank you," she said solemnly, then carefully and precisely placed it back in her pocket.

"That was a very good idea of your mummy's," Luke said, and Lucia smiled at him.

"As soon as I stopped using the pushchair, Mummy made me carry her number. She told me if I got lost not to talk to anybody in the street, but to go to the nearest shop and ask the person behind the till to phone her." She paused, looking around the shop with awe.

"I like your shop," she said. "Have you read all of these books?"

"No," replied Luke uncomfortably. "It's not my shop at all, I only work here."

"I like books very much," stated Lucia. "Have you read Charlotte's Web? It's very good," she continued, thankfully not waiting for an answer.

"We borrowed it from the library and Mummy read it to me, I loved it. I only cried a little when

Charlotte died, because of course, they don't live very long, do they?"

"Who don't?" asked Luke, a tide of bewilderment creeping over him.

"Spiders, of course," replied Lucia impatiently; fixing him with a glare that implied he should have known that.

"Do you know what my favourite colour is?" she suddenly demanded.

"Umm, pink?" Luke hazarded.

"Well, pink's my favourite colour to wear," conceded Lucia. "But my favourite colour to look at is green. My mummy's eyes are green."

Luke – experiencing whiplash from the speed the conversation changed course – manfully struggled to keep up.

"Are they?"

"Yes, the most beautiful green ever. We went to the seaside once. The water was that same sort of green. My mummy is beautiful, but she works too hard."

"Oh, that's a shame." Luke was beginning to be amused by this bright, vivacious child. "What about your daddy? What does he do?"

"I don't have a daddy."

~Chapter Two~
"There was a man..."

In an instant, the brightness in Lucia's face was extinguished, and Luke watched in dismay as her mouth quivered downwards.

"He died when I was a baby. All my grandparents are dead too, so it's just me and Mummy, oh, and Auntie Isabella."

"Who is Auntie Isabella?" asked Luke, desperate to restore the smile to her face.

"She was my daddy's sister," replied Lucia. "She's Mummy's best friend, and I like her an awful lot. I think it's important, don't you, to like your family?"

"Yes," agreed Luke, reflecting on his own diverse, widespread, and eclectic family. "It is."

The door flew open. A woman rushed into the shop in a shower of driving rain. She dropped to her knees before the child, uncaring of the state of the floor, and gathered her up in a tightly fierce embrace which moulded the young pink body to her own.

"Mummy," exclaimed Lucia in satisfaction.

Luke watched with interest as the woman held her small daughter close, took a deep, steadying breath, as if trying to inhale her child's scent, desperate to reassure herself she was there, in her arms. Finally, she rose, pushed the hood from her hair, turned, and Luke saw her for the first time.

Her eyes were green, he thought desperately, but to describe them as merely being the colour of the sea did them a severe injustice. They were that fresh, drenched green of dew-soaked grass; of waxy young buds quivering and ready to burst into life in the newness of spring. They were the colour of soft moss clinging to a tree in the still, secret places of some long-forgotten woodland.

Luke felt he could stare into them forever.

He swallowed and tried to look away, yet her air of untouched vulnerability held him fast, and he noticed other things.

The sweep of coppery hair was carelessly styled and glistening with rain droplets. It was the exact shade, he thought, stunned by his reaction to this woman, of a glass of finest cognac held up to firelight so the colour gleamed and flickered.

She was slightly built, his keen eye noticing the way the raincoat hung from her small frame, as though intended for a larger build, yet her chin was firm and determined, and he imagined it could rise proudly in an instant to face down the world.

Her features were finely drawn, her skin's warm tones suggesting a Mediterranean ancestry, and he remembered the Italian nature of the child's name.

"Thank you," she said, stepping forward, still clutching her daughter. "Thank you so much, I was so scared, I was imagining..." She broke off, flicked a glance towards Lucia and then at him.

"Well, I don't need to tell you what I was imagining."

"You don't," he agreed. "It's a very good idea to make sure Lucia carries around your number. It's a shame more parents don't think of it."

"It's the first time it's ever been tried out," she confided, with a smile in her voice, glancing proudly down at her daughter. "It's a relief to know it worked."

"It certainly did," Luke agreed; then held out his hand. "I'm Luke Blackwood, by the way."

She hesitated, then placed her hand in his. He felt the shock of contact, the smallness of her bones within his muscular grip, the softness of her skin. He also felt the strength in her grip, the slight calluses on her fingertips, and realised this was a woman who was used to hard, physical labour. His curiosity grew.

"I'm Arianna," she said. "Arianna Santorini."

Again, the name was Italian, yet the accent was British.

"You both have lovely names," Luke said curiously. "Are you Italian?"

"On my father's side," Arianna replied. "And Lucia's father was Italian, hence the surname."

Luke nodded, wondering why he so desperately wanted to keep this woman here; to keep her talking and looking at him with those amazing eyes which sparked with a lively intelligence, yet were also shadowed, as if quiet, private secrets lurked in their depths.

"Well, thank you so much again," she said. "We should go, let you get back to work."

And because he could think of no reason to delay her departure, Luke had no choice but to say goodbye and watch them go, holding up a hand as Lucia knocked on the window, frantically waving to him whilst her mother struggled to zip up her raincoat and pull up her hood against the lashing rain.

Arianna glanced up. Their eyes locked.

Luke felt a jolt like electricity, and he remained standing, staring through the window long after they had disappeared, wondering what the hell he'd got himself into now.

"So, Lucia tells me she had quite an adventure today?" Arianna glanced up at her sister-in-law's words, one slim hand pausing in its task of uncorking a bottle of wine and meeting Isabella's curious eyes, which then narrowed at the flustered, faintly embarrassed look which flashed across the other woman's face.

"What?" demanded Isabella. "What is it? What happened?"

"Nothing … happened," Arianna insisted.

"Oh, come on," Isabella persisted, her face alive with intense curiosity. "I know you too well to buy that, Anna. You might as well tell me. You know I'll get it out of you eventually."

"Well," Arianna began hesitantly. "There was a man…"

"A man?"

Isabella's voice rose in sharp surprise. Desperately, Arianna shushed her, gesturing to the door beyond which Lucia was sleeping.

Impatiently, Isabella took the corkscrew, expertly finished opening the wine and pulled her sister-in-law through the open door into the tiny courtyard garden.

The ferocious rain of the morning had ceased after lunch, and the evening had settled into weather more appropriate to summer. Now, warm enough to eat outside, the small table was already laid with pasta and salad.

"So," began Isabella, after the wine had been poured and the two women were settled in chairs facing each other.

"There was a man?" She gave an expressive gesture with her hand. "Go on."

"There's not much to tell," Arianna began, amused by Isabella's avid curiosity. "As you know, Lucia got lost, I don't know how. One minute she was beside me and the next..." Arianna shuddered and raised eyes haunted by the memory of that moment to her sister-in-law.

"I'll never forget how that felt, Bella, when I couldn't find her, I thought..."

Isabella's face sobered and she placed a hand gently over Arianna's.

"I know," she murmured. "Thank heavens it all turned out okay." She paused, and took a sip of wine, eyes sparkling with mischief. "So anyway," she persisted. "To get back to the man."

"Lucia went into his shop, the bookshop by the cinema, you know the one?"

"I do," agreed Isabella. "I've been in it many times, but I've never noticed a man in there, only the very pretty girl with the sad eyes, and the older woman who sometimes works there."

"Well," continued Arianna, sipping her wine with pleasure. "He was there today, Lucia gave him my number, he phoned me, I ran to the shop, we came home, and that's it."

"Really?" asked Isabella, smiling with delight at the colour that washed over Arianna's face.

"There is more," she breathed. "I knew it. You liked this man, didn't you?"

"We only spoke for about four minutes," protested Arianna. "There wasn't time to…"

"It only takes a second," stated Isabella firmly.

"What only takes a second?"

"Falling in love."

"Bella!" protested Arianna, half laughing, half shocked. "Honestly, I mention I found a man attractive and instantly you've got me in love."

"Ah-ha!" exclaimed Isabella in triumph. "So, you did find him attractive?"

"Well," agreed Arianna reluctantly. "He was very handsome."

"Hair?"

"Dark blond and thick."

"Build?"

"He was very tall, and big set yet not fat, just well-built, and very muscular in a tough sort of 'I can take care of myself' kind of a way, you know? And his hands were large and felt rough as if he's used to doing things with them."

"Hmm mmm," agreed Isabella dreamily. "I bet he is. Eyes?"

"Blue," said Arianna instantly, and a far-away expression passed over her face.

"The same blue the sea goes sometimes in the middle of summer when the sun glints across it and it sort of sparkles, or the way that the sky looks on hot, cloudless afternoons. He looked very kind, yet there was an element of danger about him, a sort of watchful wariness, as though he spends his life looking over his shoulder for trouble…"

Her voice trailed away at Isabella's raised brows. "My," her sister-in-law drawled wryly. "You sure did notice a lot in only four minutes."

"Oh, well, I guess when your adrenalin is up you do tend to notice things more clearly," mumbled Arianna, following suit as Isabella loaded up a fork and began to eat.

"Um huh," agreed Isabella around a mouthful of ravioli, her eyes gleaming. Arianna smiled.

For a few moments, there was silence in the small garden, the only sound the clink of cutlery and the soft chirruping of a bird in a nearby tree calling to its mate.

"Lucia asked about her father again," Arianna said when they had finished eating and were relaxing with their wine.

Isabella looked at her and carefully put down her wine glass.

"Did she?"

"Yes, she asked as I was putting her to bed. She wanted to know what he was like."

"What did you tell her?" Isabella asked quietly.

"The usual," Arianna grimaced. "I mean, what else can I tell her?"

"You could try the truth?" Isabella suggested mildly.

"The truth?" Arianna's eyes spat green fire. "Ah yes, the truth. Sweetheart, Mummy's been lying to you. Your daddy isn't dead. He is living like a lord in a South American country that doesn't have an extradition treaty with the UK. The reason he's there is because he embezzled six million pounds from the bank, he was vice president of and made his getaway, leaving us to face the music with no money, and no idea what on earth had happened!"

"Arianna," began Isabella, but Arianna clung to the side of the table and continued, eyes wide with remembered shame and past fears.

"And when he was here, he was a terrible daddy and an even worse husband, and Mummy was thinking of taking you and running away to somewhere he couldn't shout and control or bully and hurt me anymore. Because I didn't want you growing up thinking it was okay, that the way he was treating me was right. Because I was so afraid when you got old enough to answer back, that he'd stop seeing you as his little dolly princess and maybe hit you too."

She grabbed her glass and gulped at her wine. Isabella's wine glass hit the table with a thump, and she reached across and gathered up Arianna's hand in her own, soothing, and shushing, seeing how upset her sister-in-law was and the tears that threatened to well.

"I'm sorry, Anna," she whispered. "I'm so sorry, I didn't mean to bring back bad memories. I only meant Lucia's getting older, old enough to understand, and one day she may find out. After all," she continued, her voice dripping with sarcasm, "it's public knowledge what Roberto, my darling brother, did and I feel it would be better if she heard it from you first, not from someone else."

"I know," Arianna nodded. "I know, and I will tell her soon Bella, I promise. It's just …" she paused, and took another sip of wine, looking at Isabella with serious, concerned eyes.

"I want her to stay a child for as long as possible, to remain innocent. I'm scared of what the truth will do to her. I will tell her, heaven only knows how or when, but I will tell her."

~Chapter Three~
"there's something you don't see every day."

Arianna looked at her reflection in the mirror and sighed. Behind her lay almost an entire day of non-stop cleaning and she desperately needed to shower and wash her hair, but there was no time.

Lucia had gone to the all-day birthday celebration of her best friend Laura, and Arianna had taken advantage of her absence, contacted the agency she worked for and taken on three cleaning jobs, back-to-back, to fill the day.

Now she was running late. She was supposed to join them in the park at four for birthday cake and champagne for the mummies, but as it was already gone three-thirty and the park was a good fifteen minutes' walk away, she had to be content with changing into a pretty summer dress, applying make-up, and sweeping her hair up into a careless bundle on the top of her head.

As she let herself out of the flat and hurried down the road, she could already feel strands of hair escaping to gently brush her on the shoulder. Having no time to go back and fix it, Arianna merely muttered under her breath and stuffed the offending tendrils back up.

Rushing along, she reflected how cleaning other people's houses had certainly not been the way she envisioned her life going. But when Roberto left and there was no more money, Arianna had to take on a job, any job, which paid her a wage and could be juggled around Lucia's nursery and then later, school hours.

It had been tough at first, very tough. Unused to such hard, physical labour, Arianna barely survived those early days. Staggering home to the small garden flat there'd been just enough money to pay the deposit on, spending some time with her tiny daughter, then falling into bed completely worn out, sleeping nine solid hours of pure exhaustion, then heaving herself up the next morning to start the process all over again.

But gradually, things got easier. Arianna got used to the frenetic pace of her days, grew stronger, and a hard shell formed around her betrayed heart. The nights spent sobbing into her pillow over the mess she had made of her life and the treachery of her husband became a thing of the past.

Slowly, Arianna began to appreciate the little things that made her and Lucia happy.

Throughout it all, Isabella had been her staunchest supporter. Always there, giving help and encouragement, Arianna wondered how they would have coped without her.

She had once said so to Isabella, only to have her sister-in-law turn on her with fire glinting in her dark eyes.

"You're my only family," she snapped, almost annoyed, "of course I want to help, you're all I have."

Arianna smiled as she crossed the road, thinking of the extra money she had earned that day. It would go into the special bank account she had to save money for the little extras in life, the small luxuries that made the normal frugality of their existence bearable. Lucia's birthday was coming up in a month, and Arianna had earmarked the money to pay for that.

The only disadvantage of living within the catchment area of a very prestigious primary school was that Lucia's classmates tended to come from wealthy families.

Sometimes, Arianna had the unpleasant task of explaining to Lucia why they couldn't afford the holidays abroad and the expensive toys her friends had in abundance, birthdays being a classic example.

Last year, Lucia had a small select group of friends over, and Arianna assembled all the ingredients to make their own pizzas. The pampered little girls had been wide-eyed and excited with the novelty of cooking their meal, sitting in the garden to devour every, last crumb.

Afterwards, Arianna and Isabella had cleared the garden and the little girls had dressed up and danced, under rows of coloured, twinkling fairy lights, which Isabella had arrived with earlier in the day.

Lucia's party, whilst costing very little, had been the talk of the class, creating envy amongst those who hadn't been invited.

Now, Arianna was racking her brain to come up with another inspired, yet cheap, idea for Lucia's forthcoming eighth birthday.

Although things were financially easier than in the beginning, they still had to watch every penny. The situation was exacerbated by the fact she couldn't work during school holidays, other than very odd occasions like today when Lucia was cared for by someone else.

The agency was very understanding, and Arianna felt tremendous loyalty and gratitude towards them for their patience and support, and their willingness to allow her a certain degree of flexibility in the jobs she could take on.

During school hours, Arianna worked non-stop. From the beginning, she formed the habit of putting half her wages away to support them through the holidays when she was unable to work. It was a system that worked well, and she had stuck religiously to it for six years.

Checking her watch, Arianna realised she was going to be late and increased her pace, making her way down the high street to the park gates at the end.

Her eyes barely flicked left as she passed the road where the bookshop was, remembering – with a quick rush of heat – the events of two days previously, and the very handsome Luke Blackwood.

Luke was bored. It was a sluggishly hot Wednesday afternoon. As he sprawled lazily behind the counter, the sun baking him through the window, his eyelids drooped and he shook his head, desperately trying to stay awake.

He glanced at the clock. It was gone four and he hadn't seen a single customer since lunchtime. Damn it, he had had enough of this, he'd close early and go home.

Locking the door, he turned and saw her cross the end of the road, her pace brisk and purposeful. She didn't so much as glance in the direction of the shop, so didn't see him standing there.

Galvanised into action, he sped down the road and turned the corner, eyes frantically searching the crowds of afternoon shoppers before he saw her turning into the park.

Without quite knowing why, he followed, his long legs quickly gaining on her until he was forced to hang back a little, unsure of how to approach her, or what exactly to say to her.

Her hair was up today, he noticed, piled into a big, gorgeously messy bundle on the top of her head, adorable wispy strands caressing the back of her slim neck. His hands itched to simply plunge into the thick, shiny mass and slowly, ever so slowly, pull the pins out and watch the whole lot tumble down over her bare shoulders.

Luke swallowed. Where the hell had that come from? Get a grip, Blackwood, he fiercely ordered himself, you're not some hormonal teenager lusting after anything with a pulse.

Still, his eyes hungrily consumed every detail of her appearance. The simple linen shift dress fitted her slim form to perfection, its lime green colour a perfect foil to her tanned limbs and chestnut hair.

The flat, brown leather sandals with straps that crisscrossed her ankles, emphasising their slenderness. The way her hips swayed ever so slightly as she speedily walked through the park, her head occasionally turning to scan the crowds as if looking for someone.

Blackwood, you are nothing but a letch, Luke scolded himself, but couldn't look away. When she turned onto the path which led down to the lake, his feet automatically followed. Oh great, he thought wryly, now I've added stalking to my crimes.

She stopped and waved. Luke saw a group of brightly dressed women spread out on the sunlit grass, folding chairs dotted around a collection of picnic rugs, baskets, and coolers. He watched Arianna make her way across the grass towards them, greeting and being greeted in turn, saw her gratefully accept a plastic picnic flute of what looked like champagne, and settle herself into an empty chair.

Stopping by a newspaper stand, Luke bought himself a paper and sat down on a bench, noticing for the first time the group of young girls congregating by the lake. Their excited shrieks and laughter echoed back to him, and he smiled to himself when he recognised Lucia in their midst, her long dark hair pulled up high into a jaunty ponytail festooned with bright pink ribbons.

She and her friends were crowded by the lake, and Luke watched as another girl struggled with the remote control of a model boat that dashed across the surface of the water, its jerky voyage indicating the captain was unfamiliar with the controls.

"Have you all had a good day?" Arianna sipped at the delicious champagne, enjoying the welcome treat, and blinking in the strong afternoon sun.

"Very good," confirmed Jess, Laura's mother, and looked to where the girls were playing by the water's edge. Shading her eyes, she watched as her daughter wrestled with the controls of her new model boat, smiling at the exclamations and cries of the others as she grew more confident with it, sending it whirling away, executing an almost perfect turn at the far edge of the lake.

"You know," continued Jess with a smile, "when Daniel said he wanted to buy Laura a boat for her birthday I wasn't sure, but out of all the things she got, it's the one that's caused the most excitement, I mean, look at them..."

Dutifully, the other mothers looked, smiling indulgently at the pretty picture their daughters made, so shiningly young and innocent in their brightly coloured party frocks, clustered together at the water's edge, all clamouring to have a go with the new toy.

"Oh, oh, hold everything," Sam – one of the mothers – muttered, pulling her sunglasses down her nose, and looking at something over Arianna's shoulder.

"Ladies, we have ourselves one extremely fit man at six o'clock. Don't all look at once," she ordered, as every head began to swivel. "Don't want to make the poor guy paranoid. Take it in turns."

"Hmm," purred Jess, her eyes narrowing appreciatively. "Take a look at that, Arianna, there's something you don't see every day."

Amused, Arianna glanced over her shoulder, eyes widening and her mouthful of champagne almost going down the wrong way as she recognised Luke sitting on a park bench, engrossed in a newspaper, totally oblivious to the fact he was the target for some serious out and out ogling by a group of yummy mummies.

"I know him," she blurted out, then immediately wished she had kept silent as six pairs of eyes swivelled to stare at her with interest.

"Do tell," ordered Sam, topping up her glass and fixing her with an innocent stare from her big, baby blue eyes.

"Is he married, gay, or just plain weird? Because trust me, ladies, he must be one or the other. There is no way such a prime piece of man is going to be walking around single and available. Believe me, I know from bitter experience."

"I don't know much about him," muttered Arianna. "He works in the bookshop off the high street; I met him on Monday when we went in there."

"I so need to start reading more," commented Sam with a knowing look at the others, who giggled, glancing over their shoulders at Luke, sipping their champagne, each indulging in a few wistful moments of private fantasy.

~Chapter Four~
"Thank heavens you were here,"

Luke noticed the bent heads and giggles of the women, wondered what they were laughing at, then looked again with interest at the group of little girls and their efforts to get the boat to perform complicated manoeuvres around the lake.

It was a nice little model, plainly expensive, and Luke smiled at the incongruity of little girls so engrossed in a traditionally male toy, but then asked himself, why not?

The owner of the boat finally relinquished the controls to Lucia. Luke observed with a small smile his little friend's excitement at being entrusted with the command.

Carefully, she moved the controls, shrieking with joy when the boat turned as lightly as a bird and began swooping over the surface of the lake towards them.

"Make it go under the bridge," one little girl ordered. Duly Lucia twiddled the control, and the boat turned and shot under the small bridge which spanned the lake.

The girls all rushed onto the bridge, peering expectantly over the side, waiting for it to emerge, smiles slipping as moments ticked by and there was no sign of it.

"Where is it?" he heard the owner cry and saw Lucia desperately turning the buttons.

"There it is," she said, pointing to the boat snagged in weeds growing under the bridge.

"It's stuck!" the owner wailed and set off in a rush to where her mother was with all the other girls, except Lucia, chasing after her.

Luke watched in mounting horror as she carefully laid the remote down, picked up a long stick which was lying on the ground, and clambered onto the balustrade of the bridge, leaning far over as she attempted to poke the boat out from the weeds.

"No," he murmured to himself, standing up, newspaper fluttering to the ground and his heart clutching in anticipation of disaster.

Glancing at the group of mothers, he saw the little girls clustering around them, excitedly telling their tale of the maritime disaster, their bodies blocking their mothers' view of the lake, the bridge, and Lucia – who by now had realised she couldn't quite reach the boat so was leaning down, further, and further...

Luke started to run.

At the same moment, Lucia overbalanced and fell. He saw her strike her head soundly on the side of the bridge and disappear into the water with a splash.

Reaching the lake, Luke waded out into the water, its icy coldness tugging at his denim-clad thighs, struggling through the weed-choked depths to where he could see Lucia floating, her bright pink dress billowing to the surface of the murky green water.

Swiftly, he lifted her, saw the lump on her temple, and carried her back to the edge as the mothers realised something was amiss and began to rush towards him, Arianna's face a tight mask of concern as she reached the water's edge.

"Lucia!" she screamed.

Luke stepped from the lake, laying Lucia down on the warm grass. Rolling her to her side, he expertly pumped out the small amount of water she had swallowed.

Concerned she might be concussed, a vast wave of relief swept over him as her eyelids fluttered open. She focused on her mother and promptly burst into tears.

"Lucia, sweetheart!" Arianna clutched her child tightly. "What on earth did you think you were doing?" she scolded, fear and delayed panic echoing in her voice.

"I'm sorry, Mummy," stuttered Lucia, great blobby tears rolling down her cheeks. "I wanted to get the boat back."

"You could have drowned!" Arianna cried, holding her tightly to her chest, rocking her back and forth, closing her eyes in a moment of fear.

Seeing Lucia was all right, scared, and soaking wet but, all right, Luke waded back into the lake and retrieved the boat, handing it to an ashen-faced Laura, who clutched it to her chest.

"Luke, thank you, thank you so much." He looked down to see Arianna gazing up at him, green eyes luminous with almost shed tears, her face pale and drawn. "Thank heavens you were here," she continued. "Otherwise, I don't know what would have happened."

"Here," ordered Jess, handing her a picnic rug. "Wrap this around her, to keep her warm.

Gratefully, Arianna took the rug and enfolded Lucia in its sun-warmed depths, tenderly pushing the damp tendrils of hair off her daughter's face.

"I have to get you home," she murmured, struggling to her feet. She heaved Lucia into her arms, staggering under her weight.

"How far away do you live?" Luke asked.

Arianna pulled a wry face at him. "About a fifteen-minute walk," she confessed.

Luke frowned in concern. "You can't carry her all that way," he stated flatly. "You'll never make it. Look, the shop's a minute away and I have the keys to the flat above it. I'll carry Lucia back there. At least you can get her warm and dry, and we can check she doesn't have a concussion or need to go to the hospital."

"I … I don't know," began Arianna reluctantly. "It's awfully kind of you, but…"

"I think you should take Luke up on his offer," Jess stated firmly and handed Arianna her bag which she had dropped in her mad dash to the lake. "None of us came by car so we can't give you a lift home, and he's right, you'll never manage to carry Lucia all that way."

"Well, all right then," Arianna said.

Luke reached forward and took the not unsubstantial weight of Lucia into his arms, amazed her mother had even considered carrying her.

Letting them into his sister's sunny and welcoming flat a few minutes later, Luke carried Lucia into the bedroom and gently deposited her onto the bed.

"Bathroom's through there," he informed Arianna, as she followed him in. "There are clean towels in the cupboard. I'll have a root around and find some clothes for Lucia to put on."

"This is so kind of you," Arianna remarked. "Are you sure the owner wouldn't mind?"

"Of course not," Luke replied. "This is my sister Susannah's place. I know she'd be angry with me if I'd let you walk all that way home. My sister's the kind of person who collects strays," he continued, then paused as quite the ugliest ginger tomcat Arianna had ever seen, wandered into the bedroom and stared curiously at them through huge, topaz-coloured eyes.

"Hence the cat," Luke finished dryly, bending to scratch him fondly between the ears and being hissed at for his troubles. "This is Asbo," he said, and Arianna's lips twitched with amusement.

"Asbo?" she queried, as Lucia slid off the bed and held out a delighted hand to him.

"Trust me," drawled Luke. "If ever anything needed an anti-social behaviour order slapped on him, it's this moggy. Out until all hours of the night, getting into fights, disturbing the neighbourhood, I don't know why Susannah puts up with him."

The cat cast a disdainful look upwards as if he not only understood but disputed Luke's words, purring and twining himself around Lucia, who suddenly sneezed, startling Asbo and galvanising her mother into action.

"Right," she declared forcefully. "Into the shower with you, young lady."

"Just a moment," said Luke.

Kneeling before Lucia he proceeded to test her for any signs of concussion, nodding to Arianna that he was happy she seemed unharmed other than an already purpling lump on her head.

Leaving Lucia to be attended to by her mother, and after locating a long t-shirt in one of his sister's drawers, which Lucia could wear to go home in, Luke wandered into the kitchen and put a pot of coffee on to brew. He was desperate for a cup and had a feeling after the shocks of the afternoon, Arianna would probably be grateful for a cup too.

He spooned some food into Asbo's bowl, watching in amusement as the cat dived in face first, devouring the meal as if he hadn't been fed for a week, even though Luke knew full well he'd fed him only that morning.

Pushing open the charming double doors which led out onto a secluded and pretty little roof garden, Luke perched gingerly on one of the twisted wrought iron chairs, feeling the discomfort of wet denim clinging to his skin.

He stretched out his legs in the strong sunshine hoping the heat would dry the worst out and thought about Arianna Santorini.

He thought about the enticing and intriguing contrasts he sensed within her. She appeared fragile, yet she had lifted her child without a second thought. Luke knew full well if he hadn't been there, she would have carried Lucia all the way home.

Her small, delicately formed hands concealed a firm handgrip and her roughened skin hinted at hard physical labour.

Those eyes, haunting and mesmerising, pleaded for intimacy and closeness, but at the same time, he felt they pushed away, erecting barriers against the outside world.

There was movement at the doors. Arianna stepped into the garden, pausing for a moment to gaze around in delight. Luke looked at her standing there, her face tilted towards the sun in pleasure, one slim tanned hand clutching the door frame.

A shaft of pure desire lanced hotly through him. A gut blow, it took him by surprise. Hastily, he swallowed and glanced away, afraid she would look at him and see the naked need burning in his eyes.

Arianna hesitated.

Every logical cell in her brain told her to step back, get Lucia and go. Leave before she became so entangled that escape would be impossible. But escape from what ... she had no idea.

At the unfamiliar sensation of her heart pounding against her ribs, the heat rose uncontrollably to her cheeks. She had the sudden, inexplicable notion she stood poised on the brink; that something was starting right now, something over which she had no power.

She swallowed, shook her head slightly to clear such fanciful thoughts from her mind and resolutely stepped into the garden.

"This is lovely."

She heard the artificial brightness in her voice. She prayed it was only apparent to her ears how desperately hard she was trying to sound normal.

"Yes, this garden was one of the reasons Susannah bought the shop," Luke explained, wondering how she could be so unaware of the tension which sparked and crackled between them, how her voice could be so calm and even. Couldn't she feel it?

Hell, he could almost see the chemistry churning and bubbling every time he looked at her.

The soft rustle of her dress as she sat on a chair beside him and crossed her legs. The way one finger strayed absently to her hair to toy with a loose tendril, teasing and tantalising him. Round and round her finger she swirled the coppery curl until Luke's hand itched to follow suit. Resolutely, he kept his fingers firmly plastered to his side, his arms crossed in fierce denial of his body's urges.

She leant forward and he smelt her; a delicate, flowery scent that couldn't completely mask the warm, feral smell of woman underneath. He gulped, somehow managed to turn it into a cough, and then shifted away, afraid of making a complete fool of himself and alarming her in the process, hoping she wouldn't notice how her nearness was affecting him.

~Chapter Five~
"He saved my life, Mummy,"

Get a grip, Arianna sternly ordered herself, crossing and uncrossing her legs, as a strange, heavy hotness grew deep in her abdomen. She glanced surreptitiously to where Luke sat, enjoying the afternoon sun, completely oblivious to the hormonal meltdown she was experiencing beside him.

Oh, but he was gorgeous, yet it wasn't only his looks that affected her so. She had met men more handsome in her lifetime.

No, there was something about that tough, steely set to his jaw which announced to the world here was one lean, dangerous hunk of a man, take him on at your peril, offset by the warm humour in his eyes, and the compassion and courtesy he'd shown to her and Lucia.

Luke shifted slightly in his chair, and Arianna's eyes were compulsively drawn down to his legs, long and muscular in damp clinging denim.

Unwittingly her eyes trailed up the long, hardened length of him to the whipcord iron muscles of his thighs…

She snatched her gaze away, mortified, relieved her thoughts were private and that he was unaware of her arising desire.

"How's Lucia?"

He broke the silence between them. With relief, Arianna forced her errant thoughts onto the safe, practical territory of her daughter.

"She's fine," she hastily replied, flashing him a quick, tight smile. "I left her playing with the cat. Lucia loves animals," she continued, "but I'm afraid it's not practical for us to have pets."

Luke nodded, distractedly, as though he too was having trouble concentrating on the nice normal conversation they were having.

"Um, I made coffee," he blurted out, almost leaping to his feet. "I'll bring it out and see if Lucia wants anything to drink."

"Oh, thank you, although we ..." began Arianna, but he was gone, vanishing into the flat as if eager to escape her presence. Confused, she sank back into her chair, gripping its iron coolness with fingers that shook.

Long minutes later he returned, carrying a tray of coffee things, and Luke hoped the few moments spent sternly talking to himself in the kitchen had done the trick as he carefully placed the tray on the small table, and politely poured her coffee, enquiring as to her preferences.

They sipped their coffee in almost total silence, broken sporadically by generalised comments about the weather, the afternoon's events and Luke's experiences managing his sister's shop.

Finally, Arianna glanced at her watch and stood up, smiling at Luke as he too rose.

"It's getting late," she remarked. "We should go. Thank you so much, Luke, for what you did, for your kindness, I don't know what would have happened if you hadn't been there."

"I'm glad I was," Luke stated, and followed her back into the flat where they found Lucia curled up on the sofa, with a large cushion of ginger fur snuggled into her tummy.

"Get your shoes on please, sweetheart," Arianna ordered gently. Lucia struggled from the sofa and went to do her mother's bidding, leaving them alone again.

Arianna turned to bid him goodbye, holding out one slim, tanned hand which, after a second's hesitation, Luke took firmly in his own.

And it was back – the pressure, the tension, that scalding hot jolt of physical need and desire. It leapt through their clasped palms.

Luke saw with satisfaction the brief widening of her eyes, heard the low, quickly drawn in breath, realising she felt it too.

"I must go ..." she murmured, and Luke heard the panicked apprehension in her voice. "There's dinner to cook, and Lucia needs to go to bed and ... and..."

She stopped, her emotions leaping to the surface of those expressive green eyes, as Luke quietly put out a hand and did what he'd been longing to do all afternoon, stroked a stray curl back from her cheek.

They gazed at one another, his fingertips lingering warm on her face and a rosy flush cresting her cheekbones. Luke smiled, feeling her heat on his skin.

"Goodbye, Arianna Santorini," he muttered. "Until next time..."

"Um, yes, goodbye," she gulped and turned gratefully as Lucia re-entered the room, gathering up their things and hustling her daughter out the door, throwing one last agonised glance over her shoulder as they left.

Long after they had gone, Luke remained standing in the middle of the room, concerned, and baffled by the strength of the emotions which raged and raced throughout his still, silent body.

She had felt it too, of that, he was sure. A grin spread across his face.

He had no idea where she lived or what her number was, but Luke knew, could feel with every ounce of his being, that somehow, someway, he would see her again and then…

"Oh, yes, and then …" he murmured, the grin broadening as he went to clear away the coffee things and go home.

"Lucia, I don't think this is such a good idea." Arianna looked at her young daughter in exasperation. Lucia stared back stubbornly, tightening her grip on the small bunch of flame-coloured lilies.

Arianna sighed, knowing that look of old. It was a look she often saw on her face in the mirror; that determined expression that announced to the world, damn it, I will get my way.

"I want to take him flowers," Lucia repeated. "It's polite to say thank you and take flowers when someone's done something nice for you, and he did something very nice. He saved my life, Mummy," she announced melodramatically, and Arianna felt her lips twitch.

"It's only polite," Lucia stressed again, glaring at her mother. "And you've taught me to always be polite," she finished with a saintly look, knowing she'd played her trump card.

"All right then," agreed her mother. "But I'm not sure I have enough money." She peered doubtfully into her purse.

"I brought my purse with money from my piggy bank," Lucia stated firmly, and Arianna knew she had no other choice; it was game, set and match. She had been well and truly outmanoeuvred by a seven-year-old.

She watched in silence as Lucia triumphantly handed the flowers to the stallholder, waiting while he wrapped them in pretty paper, then proudly counting the money from her purse and handing it over, before taking the flowers and settling them into the crook of her arm, gazing at her mother expectantly.

"Let's go and see him now," she demanded, and Arianna hesitated.

Wait, she wanted to say, but wait for what, she was unsure. Wait, whilst she frantically whipped out a hairbrush and lipstick. Wait, whilst she tried to calm her suddenly raging heartbeat. Wait, whilst she tried to persuade her lungs to re-inflate.

Don't be so ridiculous, Arianna Santorini, she ordered herself. Unconsciously, the same stubborn look passed over her face, and as Luke had predicted, her chin rose determinedly.

"All right, though I'm still not sure this is such a good idea, Lucia," she muttered, and Lucia smiled brightly at her mother, taking her by the hand.

"Auntie Bella thought it was," she stated, and Arianna felt her eyebrows rise in enquiry.

"Did she now?" she murmured placidly, whilst thinking furiously, damn you, Bella!

Luke was busy with a customer when they entered the shop, his back to the door, and Arianna indicated to Lucia with a look that they were to wait and not interrupt.

Nodding, Lucia wandered off to the children's section and Arianna took the opportunity to quietly watch, wondering what it was about this man that had set her pulse thumping and her temperature rising, after six years of complete indifference to men.

She had been hurt, badly hurt, by the one person she should have been able to trust implicitly. Arianna knew once trust has been lost it was very difficult, if not impossible, to ever find it again.

She watched as Luke's back straightened in exasperation and could almost feel the frustrated tension emanating from him. Intrigued, she wandered closer, shamelessly eavesdropping on their conversation, and quickly realised that Luke was in trouble, big trouble.

"Young man, I simply want to know what the next book is in the series. I bought my niece the Anne of Green Gables book for Christmas. She loved it and I want to buy her the next one, but I don't know what the next one is."

The elderly lady paused, glaring at him, her expression shrewish.

"Surely you know, you must know, after all, you are working in a bookshop."

"I'm afraid I'm only covering whilst the owner is away," Luke explained patiently. "She'll be back next Monday, perhaps you could…"

"Monday's too late," interrupted the lady emphatically. "I always buy my books here and the young lady is always most helpful, most helpful!"

She broke off, glaring at Luke, her tone indicating quite clearly that he was not.

"I'm sorry..." Luke began helplessly, as Lucia took pity and came to his rescue.

"Anne of Green Gables is great," she stated, stepping forward. They turned to face her, Luke's brows shooting up in recognition.

"If you want to know what the next book is it's called Anne of Avonlea. In fact," she brandished the book triumphantly, "here it is."

"Well," exclaimed the woman and took the book, looking at it with satisfaction. "I'll take it. Thank you very much, my dear," she said to Lucia, shooting Luke an acidic look.

"Maybe you should think of applying for a job here. You certainly seem to know more than this gentleman."

Arianna watched in amusement as Luke wisely stayed silent, although his eyes twinkled at Lucia as the lady fumbled in her bag for her purse and paid for the book, before hurrying from the shop, still muttering about inefficient shop assistants.

Then he looked up and grinned at her.

Arianna's smile slipped. Whatever it was about him that had so affected her before, it was still there. She swallowed nervously, suddenly shy in his presence.

"Hello there," he said. "What a nice surprise. What are you two doing here? Apart from rescuing me from irate, elderly ladies, that is." He smiled at Lucia, who grinned back proudly.

"We've brought you a present," she replied, picking the flowers up from the floor where she had lain them and handing them to him.

Never had Arianna seen a man so surprised. He took the bunch, studied them, and then looked at Lucia with shock.

"Flowers? You bought me flowers?"

"Yes," stated Lucia, proudly. "To say thank you for saving me the other day, Teddy and I thought it was the polite thing to do." Her smile slipped slightly as he remained silent, staring from her to the brightly coloured blooms. "Don't you like them?" she demanded, her voice losing its normal confidence.

"I do," he replied. "Very much, I was surprised, that's all. I don't think anyone's ever bought me flowers before, but they're lovely, thank you."

"Thank Teddy as well," said Lucia. "It was his idea," and she shifted the soft brown bear from under her arm to wave a paw at him.

"Thank you, Teddy," said Luke, solemnly shaking the bear's somewhat tatty paw.

"Do you have a vase?" asked Lucia, taking the flowers back from him. "Because they need to go into water straight away, or else they'll start to droop."

"If you go through the door at the back of the shop," Luke told her, "you'll find a small kitchen, I'm sure there'll be some vases there, I know Susannah often has flowers in the shop so she must have some. Perhaps you could arrange them for me?" he asked, and Lucia's face brightened at the importance of the task.

~Chapter Six~
"he kissed you?"

When she'd gone, Luke turned back to Arianna. Again, she felt the full force of his gaze; those intense blue eyes with the power to see straight through her, to peel away the layers she presented to the outside world, to cut directly through to what lay buried underneath – her soul.

"She's a great kid," he commented. "You must be very proud of her."

"Oh, I am," Arianna agreed hastily. "Although, there have been moments when I would cheerfully have given her away to the first person who knocked on the door."

"You don't mean that," he said with a smile.

"No," she concurred. "I don't."

There was a silence, and then, as usually happens, they both started to speak at once.

"I wanted…"

"I was wondering if…"

They stopped, laughed, and apologised to each other.

"You go first," he ordered, and Arianna felt a hot jolt of pleasure at the warmth of his smile.

"I only wanted to thank you again for what you did the other day."

"I didn't do anything," Luke dismissed her thanks with a wave. "Well, no more than anyone else would have done."

"So, you're looking after the shop for your sister?" Arianna said, desperately making small talk, anything to fill the pulsing gap between them.

"That's right. She had a holiday booked, and then her assistant got appendicitis, so I offered to mind the store for a week. I'm kind of in-between jobs, so had nothing else to do."

Luke stopped. At his words, a look of sympathy had crossed Arianna's face.

"I'm so sorry," she breathed. "I know how horrible it is to be unemployed, to constantly be worrying about money."

Luke frowned, realised she'd misunderstood him and opened his mouth to explain. But then Lucia came back proudly carrying a vase containing the lilies, which Luke hastily took from her and stood on the counter.

"Hey, they look great," he commented. "Thank you again."

"You were going to ask me something?" Arianna said after they had all taken a moment to admire the fiery flowers. Luke looked slightly abashed, his gaze flicking from her to Lucia and then back again.

"Well," he began reluctantly. "I was wondering if maybe you'd like to come out for dinner with me one night. Nothing major," he hastily amended, seeing her eyes widen, "just, you know, a meal and a drink, or something..."

His voice trailed away at the stunned surprise on her face. Unused to caring whether a woman accepted his casually offered proposals or not,

Luke suddenly found himself caring desperately that this woman, this beautiful, proud woman say yes.

"Mummy would love to," Lucia stated firmly, ignoring her mother's gasp.

"Lucia!"

"In fact," she continued, not even glancing at her mother. "Teddy and I are having a sleepover at my best friend's house tonight." She pointed at Arianna's hand and for the first time, Luke noticed the small pink case clutched in her mother's fingers.

"So, tonight would be perfect because Mummy won't have to find a babysitter for me." She beamed innocently at her speechless mother. "We'll go and tidy the kitchen up," she announced. "We left it in a bit of a mess." Then she and Teddy made their getaway, leaving Arianna staring at Luke in stunned silence.

"I'm sorry ..." she gasped; her face flushed with embarrassment. "I don't know what to say, I apologise for my child, whom I shall be killing as soon as we get outside, and of course, I can't accept, even though it's a very kind offer, but I mean, I can't..."

"Why not?" asked Luke simply.

"Because ... well, because I..."

"Don't like me?" he said casually.

Arianna shook her head, flustered. "No, of course not, I mean, I like you, it's just..."

"You don't find me attractive?"

"I ... I ..." Arianna's voice trailed away as he stepped closer, his blue eyes intense. She watched, mesmerised, as he lifted his hand and rubbed his thumb across her bottom lip.

"Say yes," he murmured, his thumb gently rubbing, and she felt her limbs begin to dissolve like warmed cream.

"I can't…" she replied, in an agonised whisper.

"Say yes," he murmured again. His hands fastened on her arms, and he pulled her close. Her breath caught painfully in her lungs.

For long moments they simply stood, staring at one another. He saw her eyes, wide with disbelief, her soft, pink lips parted on an unspoken exclamation of surprise.

Time stopped.

He smiled a slow, lazy grin of possession, then his lips were on hers, and the shock of it rendered all further thought impossible.

Dimly, Arianna was aware they were standing in the middle of a shop in broad daylight. Anyone could simply walk in, and her daughter could come back, but she couldn't fight it, couldn't fight against herself.

Her hands crept up to rest on his chest, to push him away, somehow, instead they moved around his torso to pull him closer and still the kiss went on.

Demanding, imperious, he didn't ask, he simply took. She didn't care, instead met his demands with needs of her own, their bodies straining closer, a myriad of shocks exploding through Arianna's body which had been untouched for too long, achingly alone for so many years and so many nights.

Finally, they broke apart. She raised eyes, large with mortification, to meet his intensely serious gaze. Trembling, Arianna touched a hand wonderingly to her kiss-swollen lips, heart pounding, as he cupped her face with his large warm hands, pressing a kiss to her forehead.

"Say yes," he whispered again, and somehow, almost against her will, Arianna found herself agreeing, before jumping guiltily away from him as the door to the kitchen banged shut and Lucia came back into the shop.

"I cleared everything away," she announced.

Arianna dragged her eyes away from his and down to her daughter, praying she wouldn't notice her mother's flushed cheeks and confused eyes; couldn't hear the frantic pounding of her heart or the breath catching painfully in her chest.

"Give me your address," he murmured, pushing a pad and pen along the counter towards her. With hands that shook she wrote it down, Luke watching with a satisfied look on his face, which Lucia silently observed with a knowing smile.

"I'll pick you up at seven," he said.

Arianna frowned, suddenly remembering something. "We'll go Dutch," she offered.

Luke's eyes darkened with annoyance. "We'll do no such thing," he stated flatly.

"You're unemployed," Arianna said, and he found himself strangely touched by the concern in her voice. "I know what that's like, we go halves."

"But ..." began Luke then stopped at the steely resolve he saw in her eyes.

"We go halves, or I won't go at all," she stated firmly, and he sighed in exasperation.

"All right," he agreed. "If that's the way you want it."

She nodded, and he touched the back of her hand, a whisper of flesh against flesh. It left her trembling at the promise she felt in the contact.

"Till seven," he said, smiling as she swallowed and fled from the shop. Lucia, hurrying in her wake, flashed Luke a triumphant smile and a quick thumbs-up which made him laugh out loud.

"Oh damn, Bella, I need to talk to you, not your machine. Listen, if you pick up this message please call me immediately, it's an emergency…"

"Anna?" Isabella's concerned tones cut through her anxious voice. Arianna shifted her mobile into her other hand, fished in her bag for her keys, and hurriedly let herself into the house.

"Anna, what's wrong? Is Lucia okay?"

"Yes, Lucia's fine, but I'm not! Oh, Bella, I've done a really, stupid thing and I don't know how to get out of it … I should phone him, tell him I can't … oh, that's no good, I don't have his number. Damn, what am I going to do…?"

"What have you done?" Isabella interrupted in concern.

"I've agreed to go out with Luke for dinner tonight…"

"Luke?"

"The bookshop guy."

"Ah, that Luke. So, what's the problem?"

"The problem is, I shouldn't be…"

"Why not?"

"Has it slipped your memory that I'm still married to your brother?"

"No, you're not, the marriage ended when he buggered off to South America. Besides, you've only got six more months to go before the seven years are up and you can apply for a divorce. Anyway, we know he's probably shacked up with some other woman, so why on earth should you feel guilty about going out to dinner with a drop-dead, gorgeous guy, or wasn't he so drop-dead gorgeous following a second viewing?"

"Oh no," drawled Arianna dryly, dumping bags of shopping onto the worktop and flicking down the switch on the kettle.

"He was still gorgeous, more so than before as it happens, and when he asked me out to dinner tonight, I was shocked, speechless and I mean, of course, I said no, but then he kissed me, and somehow I found myself saying yes…"

"Whoa, whoa," demanded Isabella, her voice suddenly sharp. "Go back a step, he kissed you? I mean, what exactly are we talking about here? A quick, brotherly peck on the cheek, or a full-blown, tie me up, tie me down, and take me right now, kiss on the lips?"

There was a heavy silence; Isabella heard coffee being spooned into a pot, the clink of the spoon against a mug, and the whistle of the kettle as it began to boil.

"Anna?" she began, threateningly.

Arianna sighed. "The second option," she mumbled, wincing as Isabella gave a crow of delight.

"Really?" she shrieked. "Well, how was it?"

"It was … fine."

"Fine?"

"Yes, you know, fine."

"Anna, the weather is fine, steak and fries are fine, that cup of coffee you're making yourself is fine, but a kiss should never be described as merely fine. It's either not worth talking about, or so incredible you can't stop thinking about it. So, which was it?"

"Okay, ok," snapped Arianna, waspishly. "If you must know, it was amazing, out of this world, I had no idea a kiss could be like that… happy now?"

"Hmm," purred Isabella, satisfied. "It sounds like you are. So, what's the real problem?"

"Well, he's picking me up at seven and I don't have anything nice to wear," mumbled Arianna sheepishly, and held the phone away as Isabella's delighted laugh echoed down the line.

"Okay, that is an emergency," she agreed. "Get yourself in the shower and start making yourself more beautiful than you already are, I'll be there in half an hour."

~Chapter Seven~
"I hate men like him!"

By the time Luke rang the doorbell at seven precisely, Arianna's tension had come to a boiling point, and she was wrung out with nervous anticipation.

If she'd had any way of getting in touch with him, she would have cancelled – at least, she thought she would have done.

Although as she nervously smoothed a hand over the bronze silk shift dress which she had picked out of the six or seven outfits Bella had brought round and went to open the door, Arianna was forced to admit to herself that even if she had his number, she wouldn't have cancelled.

Taking a deep breath to steady herself, Arianna opened the door, and he was there, eyes warming with pleasure at her appearance, his gaze travelling over the simple fluid lines of the dress which suited her petite stature, making her legs appear even longer.

"Hi," he said.

Arianna smiled, ducking her head in agonies of sudden, crippling shyness, unable to meet his eyes and her knees trembling.

She noticed with some faraway part of her mind, how handsome he looked in lightweight, well-cut black trousers and a blue, open-necked silk shirt that matched the blue of his eyes exactly.

"Come in," she stuttered. "I just need to get my things."

"There's no rush," he answered, following her in and closing the door behind him. "The table isn't booked until eight, and as the restaurant's only a ten-minute walk away, I thought we could have a drink first." He held up a bottle of chilled white wine.

"Where are we eating?" she asked, stretching to reach the cupboard where she kept the glasses.

"Alessandro's," he replied, expertly taking the corkscrew she passed him and opening the bottle with one smooth movement.

"Oh, it's lovely there," Arianna agreed in genuine pleasure. "Isabella, my... friend, took me there for my birthday last year and I enjoyed it very much."

There was silence as he poured the golden liquid into the glasses and handed her one, gently touching the side of her glass with his own, before looking around her home curiously.

He realised from the two bells on the front door of the typical, Victorian terraced house, that it was split into two separate dwellings, and that Arianna and Lucia lived in the bottom half.

As she led him along the communal hallway, he noticed the door at the foot of the staircase, saw it had a Yale lock and was clearly the door to the upstairs flat. Then she was leading him through a door on the left into her flat, closing the door behind them.

His first impression was how small it was, his second, was how charming and cosy. It reminded him of his grandmother's house, the layout typical of houses from the Victorian period.

Standing in the kitchen, he looked back into the room he'd first entered, noting the cast iron fireplace, the small table, and chairs in front of the window, and the deep inviting sofa.

There were small but stylish touches everywhere reflecting Arianna's personality – attractive cushions, fresh flowers in the fireplace and unframed black and white photos grouped randomly on the walls.

The back door was open letting the warmth and peace of the evening seep into the house, and Luke found himself being drawn to the outside, seeing the pretty, blue, painted wooden window boxes on the deep outside sills of the lounge and kitchen windows, and the wooden bench facing the back door, surrounded by pots and tubs of fresh green herbs and fragrant flowers.

"Would you like to sit outside for a while?" Arianna asked.

Luke agreed, keen to see more, looking around with interest as he followed her down the side of the house into the small, pretty courtyard garden, sitting on one of the wooden chairs and placing his glass carefully on the table.

"This is charming," he stated, looking around at the lush green oasis.

"Thank you," Arianna replied, clearly pleased. "I know it's only small, but it's so nice to have some outdoor space in the city. Do you have a garden?"

"Not really," he said. "Just a balcony."

"Oh well, even a small balcony can be made lovely with pots and things," she reassured him, and Luke nodded, reflecting how her entire flat would fit onto his balcony with room to spare.

The restaurant was small but intimate, and Arianna looked around with pleasure as they were shown to their table, strategically placed by open doors which led onto a small courtyard in which a fountain bubbled merrily, and strings of small white lights twinkled from the trees.

"This is lovely," exclaimed Arianna, taking her menu from the waiter and looking around her with pleasure.

Luke smiled in reply, thinking of the phone call he'd made earlier to his old friend Alessandro, arranging to have the best table in the house, and paying a large part of the bill in advance, in case Arianna insisted on her ridiculous idea of going halves.

She studied the menu, a small frown tugging at her forehead. Luke watched in fascination, wondering if she realised how expressive her face was.

He knew, without her having to say anything, she was worried about the prices, wondering if she could afford them, probably wondering if he could afford them as well.

Luke had noticed her home, charming and cosy as it was, had displayed no obvious signs of Arianna having much disposable income. Besides, she was a single mother. That alone was a drain on anyone's earnings.

So, he cleared his throat and prepared to tell her the truth.

"Arianna."

She glanced up at him and smiled. "Yes?"

"There's something I need to tell you, I'm afraid I haven't been completely honest with you?"

"Oh?" She still smiled, yet Luke could sense the sudden caution behind her eyes.

He swallowed, thinking how best to frame the words when there was a disturbance at the front of the restaurant.

"What do you mean you haven't got a table?"

As one, heads turned to see who was complaining in such a loud voice. Arianna, craning her neck, saw a man, bluff and portly, his clothes and bearing demanding attention and proclaiming to all who saw him, here stood an extremely wealthy man who was used to getting his way.

"Pardon me, sir," Alessandro himself had emerged from the kitchen to deal with the emergency, his kindly face creased with concern. "But I am afraid, without a reservation..."

"Reservation? How dare you, do you know who I am?" the man demanded. Beside him, Arianna saw a woman, whom she took to be his wife, wince in excruciating embarrassment.

"Donald," she murmured, her face flaming under all the interested stares of the other diners. "Please, don't make a fuss, let's go somewhere else."

"Don't make a fuss? Of course, I'm going to make a fuss! You said you wanted to go to Alessandro's for dinner as it's your birthday today, so here we are."

"It is your birthday, Madam?" Alessandro asked.

"Yes," the woman nodded. "But I thought he booked, I'm so sorry. If I'd realised…"

"Stop apologising, Millie!" snapped the man, and the woman subsided, her face miserable. "Look," continued the man. "How much extra do you want to fit us in?"

"It is not a question of money, sir…"

"It's always a question of money!" stated the man flatly.

"Perhaps you would care to have a celebratory glass of champagne in the garden, on the house of course," Alessandro put in hastily, seeing the man about to object. "We will bring you some menus, and I will see about squeezing you in somewhere as a favour to Madam."

"Thank you so much," whispered the poor woman.

Alessandro bowed formally. "A beautiful woman should never be allowed to go hungry on her birthday," he stated chivalrously, and the woman went pink with pleasure.

Luke watched with mild curiosity as the man and woman sat in the garden, drinking their free glasses of champagne, and studying the menu whilst the waiters quickly moved a display of plants and magically produced a charmingly intimate table for two in the corner.

"See," he heard the man state confidently to his wife as they were led past to their table. "Throw enough money at someone and they'll always give in."

Luke knew Alessandro of old, knew he fitted the couple in for the woman's sake because he felt sorry for her, not because her husband had offered him money.

Luke also knew, when the final bill was presented, it would be for precisely the amount their meal had come to, not a penny more, not a penny less.

He turned to speak to Arianna and saw her face, saw the rage that boiled and churned beneath its smooth surface.

"What's the matter?" he asked, concerned.

"I hate men like him!" she spat in a furious whisper. "Rich, arrogant, inconsiderate men who think because they've got money it gives them the right to walk all over everybody else. His poor wife, I bet he's a monster to live with. Money!"

She paused, and took an angry gulp of wine, her eyes flicking up to meet Luke's surprised gaze.

"I'm sorry," she said, and Luke saw her visibly pull herself together, taking deep, calming breaths.

"I'm sorry," she said again. "You must think I'm very strange, reacting like that. It's just, that my husband was like that, at least that's how he was when he became wealthy. When I met him, he was kind and sweet and considerate, until he got some money. Then he changed almost overnight, became petty and vindictive, and always had to be in control." She smiled ruefully.

"I guess that's why I vowed to myself never to become involved with a wealthy man again. Stick to poor but honest ones, that's what I always say." She touched her glass to his and took a sip of wine.

"So," she continued, placing her glass down and fixing her attention on him. "What was it you wanted to confess to me?"

"Um," Luke paused, his heart sinking within his chest, unsure what to say. "Oh, only that you seemed to get the idea when I told you I was in-between jobs, it meant I was unemployed. I'm not, what I meant was, I was injured in my job and had to take some time off to recover, but the job's still waiting for me."

"Oh," replied Arianna, and her face brightened. "Well, that's a relief, I know how horrible it is to be unemployed and have no money."

"What happened?" Luke asked, desperate to steer the conversation away from him.

"The usual," Arianna shrugged. "Suddenly there was no more marriage and no more money. I was a bit stuck, to be frank, no savings, no qualifications, and a young child to look after."

"Your husband had made no provision for you both in the event of his death?"

"What?" Arianna looked at him, seemingly confused.

"Lucia told me her father was dead," Luke replied gently and wondered at the look that briefly flashed into Arianna's eyes.

~Chapter Eight~
"Family is important,"

Arianna blushed. "Yes, of course, he's dead, but no, there was no money, only debt."

"That's a tough situation for anyone to find themselves in. What did you do?" Luke leant towards her, interested.

"Oh, this and that," Arianna replied.

Luke gently took her hands and turned them over, his fingers rubbing softly at her hardened fingertips.

"I know you work hard, Arianna," he stated quietly. "That's nothing to be ashamed of."

"I'm not ashamed," she snapped, flushing slightly. "I'm a cleaner, so what? Okay, it's not exactly how I saw my life going, and I know it's not what my parents would have wanted for me. But I had no choice; I had to get a job, any sort of job that paid me a wage I could live on and take care of Lucia. It's worked out pretty well. The agency knows I have to work around her school times, so I'm always there for her."

She stopped, staring almost defiantly at Luke, and he felt his heart constrict at the strength he saw in her eyes.

Slowly, he raised her hand to his mouth and planted a warm kiss on her palm.

"Arianna Santorini," he said. "You are probably the most amazing woman I've ever met."

They walked home slowly in the dusky evening, still wrapped in the intimacy that a good meal in a warm and friendly Italian restaurant and a bottle of wine can engender.

Luke was happy because, in the end, Arianna had let him pay the bill. Although she opened her bag as if to reach for her purse, she then seemed to change her mind, and Luke was relieved he hadn't had to insist after all.

Arianna's heart pounded with mortification. She wondered if Luke had noticed, or if she managed to get her bag shut in time. Or rather, if she managed to get the bag which Isabella had insisted on lending her, shut in time.

The same bag she transferred the essentials from Arianna's normal bag into, whilst Arianna had been finishing her make-up.

A bag Isabella gaily snapped shut and handed to her, before slipping out of the house only minutes before Luke was due to arrive.

A bag that now had a small, cellophane-wrapped box of condoms sitting prominently at the very top.

Damn you, Bella! Arianna thought furiously, chewing on her lip, and casting agonised glances at Luke. Had he seen? Oh, if he had, she would die of embarrassment, but not before she'd killed Bella.

And there was the question of the bill. She'd promised to go halves, and then at the last minute – terrified if she tried to get her purse out the condoms would catapult across the restaurant – she'd simply closed her bag and not said anything, allowing Luke to get the bill. Although come to think of it, he had looked quite pleased about it.

They reached her front door and Arianna paused, unsure of the etiquette of the moment. Having never been on a date before, she didn't know if it was obligatory to ask him in for coffee, or whether one simply said goodbye on the doorstep.

Luke sensed her confusion. He was an honourable man, usually, but didn't hesitate to take full advantage of it by simply taking her keys from her hand and unlocking the door, ushering her into the dimly lit hallway, achingly aware of her scent and her closeness as he had been throughout the entire meal.

He walked her to her flat's door, gave back her keys, and watched her unlock the door. He knew he should be a gentleman, should say goodnight and go, but he didn't want to.

He didn't want the evening to end and intended to squeeze out every second of being with her. So, he followed her into her flat, made cosy and inviting by the lamps she had left on.

"Thank you," she stuttered, her heart threatening to choke her to death. "For the meal and the evening, it's been…"

He nodded, his eyes warm on her face and Arianna swallowed hard, completely at sea. Having had no experience of inviting men back after a date, or even for that matter, dating, she had no idea what happened next.

"Coffee?" she whispered, desperately trying to remain calm.

"That would be nice," he replied. His eyes never left her face, and she took a reluctant step back, then another, until she bumped into the door frame and the kitchen was behind her.

Busying herself spooning coffee into the pot, and getting out her best mugs, milk, and sugar, she was intensely aware of him all the time.

Luke knew he flustered Arianna and found it touching the way her eyes spoke the words her lips couldn't bring themselves to.

Watching her make coffee, her movements measured and precise, he still saw the way her hands shook, and the quick, nervous swallow she took.

Wanting to ease the intensity of the moment, he searched for something to say.

"It's still a lovely evening, shall we have coffee in the garden?"

"Sorry? Oh, yes, of course," Arianne flashed him a quick smile that lit fireworks in his heart. "If you flick that switch by the back door, that one, that's right, it'll switch on the garden lights."

Obeying her instructions, Luke then opened the back door and took the tray of coffee things from her, following her out into the still, starry night, admiring the twinkling lights that now illuminated the tiny space, turning it into a magical oasis.

"Very pretty," he said, making a mental note to maybe see about getting some twinkly lights for his balcony.

"Bella bought them last year for Lucia's birthday present."

"Bella?"

"Isabella, my sister-in-law, she's Roberto's sister and after he ... well, she stayed in touch and has been simply amazing, so supportive. I honestly don't know what we'd have done without her."

"Family is important," he agreed.

For some reason, Susannah's sad face flashed before his eyes. She was deeply unhappy, he knew, her marriage break-up had hit her hard. Had he been as supportive as he could have been? Luke determined when she returned from holiday, to spend more time with his sister, to do what he could to help her.

They sat at the small wooden table they had sat at earlier. Arianna poured them coffee, and Luke suddenly thought how right this all felt. Being here, now, with this woman, it was almost as if it was meant to be. As if he had been waiting all his life, just for her.

Silence fell. But it was a good silence. Relaxing and accepting, Luke breathed deeply of the night air, his senses on full alert.

He could see the flush on Arianna's cheeks as she buried her face in her coffee, shy and uncertain.

He could hear the tinkling of running water somewhere and briefly thought there must be a water feature buried beneath the foliage.

He could feel the pounding of his heart as it thrust against his ribs, demanding attention.

He could taste the excellent coffee, strong and rich on his tongue.

And he could smell her perfume, subtle and understated, yet still enticing.

Reaching out, he lay a large, strong hand over her slight one, gently massaging her fingers, feeling their fragility and strength beneath his touch. Startled, she looked up straight into his eyes. The moon held its breath.

And Arianna was lost, helplessly and hopelessly, realising she never had a chance. Ever since she met this man, they had been hurtling towards one inevitable conclusion. He leant towards her.

Unaware of her movement, she met him halfway, their faces almost touching, then he brought his forehead to hers, his hand gently stroking her cheek.

She sighed against his mouth, and Luke felt her surrender; felt the sweetness of her small hands creeping up around his neck, pulling him closer. In the dimness, he saw her beautiful eyes sweep closed as the kiss deepened.

Never had Arianna felt this way before, this desperate, all-encompassing desire to have and hold and touch and taste. The kiss deepened, his hands pulling her closer, closer, the arm of her chair pressing into her stomach as she twisted herself further into his embrace.

The kiss ended, and they broke apart, gasping for air. Arianna lay back in her chair, her hand to her chest, fingers splayed over her frantically pounding heart.

With huge, dark eyes, she looked at him, and Luke suddenly wished she would look at him that way, every day, for the rest of his life.

"Arianna," he croaked, voice hoarse with emotion.

Arianna shook her head, unable to stop herself, unable to believe what she was doing. Her fingers went to his mouth to stop his words. A satisfied smile pouting her lips, she moved closer, laying her head on his shoulder, and felt his strong arm encircle her, hugging her close.

Luke dropped a light kiss to the shining head now nestled into his neck, then rested his cheek on her soft hair. Sighing, Arianna put her arm around his waist and sensed rather than felt his wince of pain.

Curiously, she pulled back and looked up at him, her eyes searching, her brow knitting in a frown of concern.

"Are you all right?" she murmured, hand hovering as if afraid to touch again in case it hurt.

"I told you I was injured at work," he began. "Well, that's the injury."

"Did you fall or something?" she asked in concern.

Luke hesitated, then tugged his shirt out, pulling it up so she could see his side, the jagged, freshly healing scar, and the still visible stitches.

Arianna swallowed, horrified. Obviously, he had been badly hurt, yet some small part of her brain still took the time to register his toned abdomen and the smoothness of his skin.

"Oh, my goodness," she exclaimed, shocked. "I thought you meant you'd hurt your back or something, not ... what is that? It looks as though someone stabbed you!"

"They did," Luke drawled wryly.

Arianna's startled eyes flew to his. "What, exactly, is it you do?" she asked, slowly.

Luke hesitated, wondering how much to tell her, wondering how deeply entrenched her aversion to wealthy men was.

"I work for an organisation called ICRA," he finally said.

"ICRA? What's that? What does it do?"

"It's the International Child Recovery Agency and it does exactly what it says on the tin. We recover lost children, mostly those snatched by estranged parents and taken abroad. We track them down, recover them by whatever means necessary and bring them back."

Arianna's eyes were as wide as saucers and she shook her head, plainly at a loss for words.

"I see," she finally said. "How did you get stabbed then? Is it very dangerous?"

"Not usually," Luke reassured her, and she shook her head again, her eyes clouded with concern, then bit her lip and looked away as though considering what to say next.

"I haven't been entirely honest with you, Luke," she began, hesitantly. She pulled away from him, sitting upright in her chair, turning to face him, her expression serious.

"There's something you need to know, something I have to tell you." She paused and sighed.

~Chapter Nine~
"How was the sex?"

Luke's heart clutched with anxiety. "What is it?" he asked carefully.

"Lucia's father didn't die," Arianna replied, quietly. "He left us six and a half years ago, and I haven't seen or heard from him since. I let her believe he's dead because, well, because it seemed easier that way."

Now it was Luke's turn to be at a loss for words and he stared at Arianna, seeing the guilty misery in her eyes.

"Do you know where he is?" he finally asked.

Arianna shrugged. "South America, I believe," she replied. "It doesn't matter, I know he's never coming back, and even if he did, I want nothing more to do with him."

"Because he abandoned you," Luke began. "I understand..."

"No," Arianna snapped. "You don't understand at all. Even if he hadn't left us, I was planning on leaving him. When I married Roberto, he was the kindest, sweetest man I'd ever met, but within a year he'd changed into an arrogant, cruel, and manipulative bully.

"His parents died before we met and he inherited a substantial sum from them, then he started working for Bank Italia and began earning a very good salary. It changed him, the money, it completely changed him.

"He became someone who thought it was okay to abuse his wife, and I was so afraid he'd begin mistreating Lucia as well..."

She looked at Luke, her chin raised.

"That's why I can't bear wealthy men," she stated decisively. "And that's why I vowed to never again become involved with anyone who has so much money they think it gives them the right to control others."

Luke's heart sank as he silently studied her, realising she meant every single word.

"She thinks you're what?" Marcus Blackwood leant back in his plush leather chair, steepled his fingers, and stared over them, eyes narrowed, at his younger half-brother.

"Poor," said Luke, sheepishly, squirming under his brother's stunned gaze.

"Poor?" repeated Marcus, incredulously.

"Well, not poor as in living in a cardboard box," Luke hurriedly amended. "I mean poor as in not rich."

His brother snorted in amusement. "I'm curious," he said. "What is it she thinks you do then?"

"Oh, she knows I work for ICRA," replied Luke.

"Just not that you own it?"

"No..."

"And I take it she also has no idea you're one of the Blackwood heirs, and that when our father died three years ago you inherited a one-tenth share of his not insubstantial fortune?"

"Umm, no," Luke grimaced. "I kind of didn't tell her that either."

"What is it exactly that she has against wealthy men? I mean, for most women it's a definite tick in the desirable attributes box."

"Not for Arianna," Luke sighed. "From what I can gather this ex-husband of hers did such a number on her, she doesn't trust any wealthy man not to be controlling and manipulative. A bully in other words."

His brother snorted again. "She doesn't know you very well then. You're about the least controlling person I know. Look at how Susannah and Marina twist you around their little fingers."

Luke opened his mouth to disagree, to protest he only cared for his sister and mother in the way any man of the household would, but Marcus had already moved on.

"Roberto Santorini," he mused. "Now why does that name sound so familiar?"

Luke watched Marcus furrow his brow in thought, glancing around as the door to his brother's plush office silently opened and Sally, Marcus's frighteningly efficient PA, quietly entered bearing a tray of coffee things which she placed on the desk between them.

"Roberto Santorini," Marcus repeated.

Sally glanced up, one brow lifting in enquiry, the light from the large, plate-glass window reflecting the auburn highlights in her sleek, neat cap of hair. Luke noted the pristine, cream silk blouse tucked perfectly into her trim, black pencil skirt, the shapely legs ending in immaculate, black, patent leather heels.

Not for the first time he wondered about his brother and his highly polished PA, then reflected as Sally wasn't human – no real woman could look that perfect or be that efficient, all the time – his brother probably considered her the way he did his laptop.

"Roberto Santorini?" she enquired curiously, adroitly pouring coffee, steaming hot and fragrant, into two porcelain cups. "Don't tell me they finally managed to get extradition for him?"

"What?" Luke turned startled eyes up to Sally.

"Have you heard of him, Sally?" Marcus asked.

"Of course," she replied. "Roberto Santorini, if it's the same person, was the man who defrauded Bank Italia of six million pounds before disappearing to South America."

"I knew the name was familiar," declared Marcus. "But I don't remember the details…"

"Well, you were busy in the New York office when it happened," stated Sally. "By the time you returned, most of the fuss had died down."

"Can you tell us what happened please, Sally?" pleaded Luke.

Sally pursed her neat mouth, copper-coloured lipstick matching exactly the shade on her immaculately manicured nails, which in turn picked out precisely the colour in her hair.

"It happened about six years ago, maybe a little more. I remember it shook the banking community quite considerably that someone so highly placed and respected could do such a thing. Although, there had been rumours before that Santorini was a bad lot. I remember feeling so sorry for his poor wife."

"Arianna," murmured Luke.

"Yes," agreed Sally, in surprise. "I believe that was her name, I saw her on TV once or twice. For a while, they suspected she had been a part of it.

I think they probably gave her a hard time," she paused, shaking her head sadly.

"She was so very young and there was a baby. Anyway, after a while, they realised she was innocent of any involvement, but I imagine it must have been unpleasant for her. Something like that must leave long and lasting scars."

"It did," muttered Luke, under his breath.

"Thank you, Sally," said Marcus as she placed the cups in front of them.

Sally flashed him a neat smile and turned to go, pausing at the door to turn and look meaningfully at Luke.

"To go through such an experience … well, it would make a woman very mistrustful," she began, and both men looked at her curiously.

"For a woman like Arianna Santorini to ever believe in a man again, that man would have to be very understanding and completely honest with her, or else it would merely reinforce her conviction that all men are cowardly liars."

She raised her brows at Luke as if enough had been said, and slipped neatly from the room, closing the door silently behind her.

There was a long silence, and then Luke sighed and looked at his brother.

"Is your PA a witch?" he enquired mildly.

Marcus grinned, amused.

"Probably," he agreed. "But she has a mind like a computer, her filing system is legendary, and her coffee is always superb," he paused to take an appreciative sip, "and sometimes she brings in homemade chocolate chip cookies which defy description."

A wistful expression settled over his face.

"A man could forgive a lot for a taste of those cookies," he murmured.

"So, what do you think I should do?"

"Do?"

"About Arianna," demanded Luke. "About the fact she thinks I'm a normal, poor but honest kind of guy, and about the fact if she ever found out I'm …" he paused and shrugged.

"Disgustingly rich …" added his brother, helpfully. Luke glared at him.

"It sounds to me," Marcus continued, "as if she's not the type of woman who wants a meaningless, no strings attached, fling. If that's all you're interested in, I think you should leave well enough alone."

"It's not all I'm interested in," denied Luke hotly. "Arianna's different, she's special. I know I could hurt her and that's the last thing I want to do. But she's so vulnerable, and if she ever finds out I've lied to her, or worse, that I *am* one of those rich, arrogant bastards she so detests, then I'll lose her and…" He paused, looking steadily at Marcus. "I'm not sure I could bear that," he finished quietly.

His brother saw the truth on his face and dropped his cup in the saucer with a thump, leaning forward in his chair with a speculative gleam in his eyes. "You're in love with her," he stated, almost accusingly.

"No, I'm not," insisted Luke. "I mean, it's impossible, I've only known her a few days…"

"It only takes a moment." His brother unconsciously echoed Isabella's words and smiled at Luke's instinctive recoil.

"So, how was the sex?" Marcus asked casually, his smile deepening as Luke's head snapped up, an angry flush on his face.

"None of your damn business!" he snapped.

Marcus grinned like the proverbial Cheshire cat. "Ah, so you haven't slept with her yet. Oh, definitely in love," he stated, with an air of almost palpable smugness.

Luke glared darkly at him, but his brother completely ignored him. Taking another slurp of coffee, he reached for a biscuit, raising a brow in enquiry. "When are you seeing her again?"

"Tonight." Luke decided to forgive his brother, swiping a biscuit before they all went. "She's invited me to dinner to meet her sister-in-law, Isabella."

"Meeting the family already?" chortled Marcus. "Don't try to deny or fight against it, little brother. It's official. You're the first of the Blackwood boys to fall."

"Well," drawled Isabella dryly, her gaze sweeping over Arianna. "You look ... satisfied."

Arianna glared at her sister-in-law, who stood poised in the front doorway, one hand tapping blunt, highly polished nails against the frame, a knowing smile quirking her beautiful face.

"Shh," hissed Arianna, casting an agonised glance back towards the flat where Lucia was watching TV, then pulling Isabella through the front door, letting it close behind her with a thump, before scuttling back down the hall into the flat, leaving Isabella to follow, brows raised, the smile now twitching at her lips.

"Auntie Bella," cried Lucia, and ran across the room to launch herself into her arms.

"Hi, there, kid." Isabella returned the hug, her eyes closing as she breathed in the sweet smell of the child, thinking how she'd do anything, literally *anything*, to ensure this precious, small family of hers remained safe and happy.

"So," she whispered to Lucia, cuddling her on the sofa and casting a glance at Arianna happily oblivious at the stove in the kitchen, her back to them, stirring something in a pan.

"How's the plan going?"

"Really, *really* well," Lucia whispered back, her eyes full of conspiratorial mischief. "Your idea about the flowers worked. Thanks for lending me the money to buy them."

"No problem," Isabella shrugged. "It was for a good cause. I take it you did leave them alone for a while?"

"Yes, I think he kissed her or something cos when I came back, Mummy's eyes were all funny, sort of mushy and dreamy and she'd agreed to go out with him. They went out last night, and ever since she's been so happy. When she had her shower this evening, I could hear her singing, and you know Mummy only ever sings when she's mega happy."

"Hmm," agreed Isabella in satisfaction. "That is a good sign. Now, you know what to do this evening, don't you?"

"Yes, I..." began Lucia then shut her mouth with a snap as Arianna came back into the room, looking at their bright eyes and grinning faces with a suspicious smile of her own.

"What are you two whispering about?" she demanded. Isabella and Lucia exchanged glances, before chorusing together.

"Nothing."

~Chapter Ten~
"I like you, Luke Blackwood,"

Arianna frowned, then practically leapt in the air as the doorbell went, Isabella noting with intense interest the flush which raced over her cheekbones and the way her hand flew to her chest as if trying to still a suddenly raging heartbeat.

"That'll be Luke," was all she said though, and Isabella marvelled at her calmness.

"I'll go," shrieked Lucia, and shot from the room leaving Isabella surveying her sister-in-law with satisfaction.

"That good, hey?" she enquired casually.

Arianna blushed and swallowed. "Oh, Bella," she muttered. "I think I'm in trouble."

"I think so too," replied Isabella with a smile. "But believe me, it's the best kind of trouble to be in," and laughed aloud at the consternation on Arianna's face.

After only five minutes spent in his presence, Isabella Santorini had summed Luke Blackwood up as being exactly the kind of man she was happy for her sister-in-law and best friend, to fall in love with. Because Arianna *was* in love.

Deny it she might. Perhaps hadn't even realised it herself, but to an outsider keenly watching the body language, shared looks and other subtle, but oh so telling signs, it was clear, not only that Arianna loved, but was loved in return.

It was obvious from Luke's dazed expression every time he looked at her – the way his fingers constantly sought excuses to touch her, and his small, courteous gestures – that Luke Blackwood was a man, if not all the way gone in love, at least halfway there.

She liked him, Isabella decided, inwardly breathing a sigh of relief.

She had struggled long and hard with her conscience before deciding to interfere in the smallest of ways and arrange for Arianna to meet him again.

After all, he was the first man to raise even a flicker of interest in six, very long years, during which Isabella had watched with dismayed admiration as Arianna put her life on hold, dedicating herself solely to the care and well-being of her child.

Not that Isabella in any way failed to understand, of course not, Lucia was supremely special. In Arianna's place, she'd have done the same, but it *had* been six years.

Lucia was beginning to relish a little independence, to not need her mother quite so much and, in Isabella's mind anyway, it was high time Arianna thought of herself and her own needs.

It was a very satisfied Isabella who leant back in her garden chair, gratefully accepting the glass of Merlot Luke passed to her, raising her eyebrows at the quality of the wine.

She knew Arianna would have no idea that the wine he thoughtfully brought with him probably retailed at upwards of twenty pounds.

Luke, meanwhile, had to admit his preconceptions about Isabella Santorini had been way off base; that his mental picture of an older, motherly type fussing over her abandoned younger sister-in-law was about as wrong as it could be.

Firstly, Isabella Santorini was the same age, if not younger than Arianna. Secondly, she was stunning. Her sleek, cropped black hair, framed a strong tanned face whose mouth could be considered too generous for beauty, cheekbones so high they appeared glacial, and eyes so dark they were almost sinister, yet somehow, put them all together and the result was a woman who could stop traffic.

Add to that, a tall, well-toned body showcased in stylish, beautifully cut clothes, and Luke concluded she was a woman who earned enough money to satisfy her desire for designer wear, as well as one who clearly worked out regularly and religiously to maintain such a superb physique.

For all her superficial attractions though, Luke quickly realised Isabella had a heart more than capable of love and generosity.

As he watched the small family of three interacting, their ease with each other speaking of years of loving intimacy, he felt grateful that through all the tough times, Arianna had had such a loyal and loving friend.

They ate in the garden – something homecooked, Italian and utterly delicious – yet Luke couldn't have told you what it was he was eating, his whole being, his entire soul, being consumed with one thought – Arianna.

She was even more beautiful than he remembered; her soft, tawny hair glowed in the late evening sun, and her face flushed with the pleasure of having her loved ones gathered around.

Her eyes, those amazing green eyes which were incapable of hiding her emotions, frequently met his in an anticipation of emotion, and he longed to be alone with her, to hold her in his arms and show her everything he was feeling in his heart.

The meal over, Arianna informed Lucia it was time for bed, rather surprised when she agreed immediately, almost eagerly, rather than the protests Arianna had been anticipating.

Hugging and kissing her aunt goodnight, only Luke caught the look and the ghost of a wink that passed between them.

Briefly, he wondered, then Lucia was flashing him a bright smile and wishing him a goodnight, before vanishing into the house with her mother, leaving him and Isabella alone in the small, peaceful garden.

"So," Isabella drained her glass, held it out for a refill and fixed him with a coolly level gaze.

"I take it Anna has no idea you're a multi-millionaire?"

Luke jolted, spilling ruby red wine over the tablecloth, his startled eyes leaping to Isabella's amused face.

Buying himself time, he dabbed frantically at the spreading stain with his napkin, before picking up the bottle and refilling her glass. After a second's pause, he also filled his own. Hell, he had a feeling he was going to need it.

"For the past six years, Arianna has become rather insular. Understandably, her main concern has been survival, not only her own but also her child's," Isabella began, twirling her glass thoughtfully in her fingers. "The name Blackwood meant nothing to her, but it did to me." She paused, fixing him with a steely glare.

"It's been hard for her. She wouldn't accept any financial aid from me, even though it was my bastard of a brother who'd placed her in such a tenuous position." She eyed him steadily. "I'm assuming you've already found out precisely who, or rather, what, my brother was?"

"Roberto Santorini?" Luke slowly nodded. "Yes, I know he defrauded Bank Italia of a quite considerable sum of money and then absconded, leaving Arianna to face the music."

"The police raked her over the coals refusing to believe she could be so naïve, could genuinely have had no idea what he'd been planning, that it wasn't some kind of scheme cooked up between them and that she wouldn't be joining him sometime in the future."

Isabella shook her head, eyes darkening at the memory of those long ago, but far from forgotten, days.

"It nearly destroyed her. A weaker woman would have been. But in case you haven't realised it yet, Arianna's stronger than she looks, and she had Lucia to focus on. When the police finally accepted her innocence, although I know they continued to monitor her activities for years, Arianna pulled herself together and took on cleaning jobs, anything she could get that fitted in around Lucia's nursery, and then school times. It broke my heart having to watch her go out to clean other people's houses, yet in time I came to realise Arianna didn't see it that way."

"It's nothing to be ashamed of," broke in Luke, hotly. "Being paid for honest work, it's nothing to be ashamed of…"

"It's not," Isabella agreed. "And I admire Anna more than any woman I know, because she had the guts, the balls if you like, to drag herself out from the pit and create a clean decent life for herself and Lucia, one that wasn't tainted by my brother's evilness."

"You really don't like him, do you?" Luke asked, fascinated by the flash of hatred he saw in those dark eyes.

"No," Isabella took a deep breath and an even deeper slug of wine. "No, I hated him long before he married a young, naïve girl and set about trying to break her. I despised him." She looked Luke straight in the eye and he was struck by the candour he saw.

"But anyway," she continued, and he sensed the door being closed on the subject, "that's not what I wanted to talk to you about. I wanted to know how you intend to get around the very real problem that once Anna discovers who you are, she will more than likely reject you?"

Isabella's voice rang out clearly in the still evening air, and instinctively Luke glanced towards the house.

"Don't worry," Isabella reassured him. "Lucia's keeping her occupied. We already arranged it so I could have this little … chat, with you."

"I see," replied Luke, understanding now the conspiratorial wink he noticed earlier between Lucia and her most unconventional aunt.

"So," Isabella sipped delicately at her wine, her eyebrows arching with pleasure.

"Which Blackwood are you? The business mogul, the one who rescues snatched kids, or the war photographer that seems to have been born with a death wish?"

"Liam?" Luke confirmed with a wry grin. "You've got that part right. He regularly gives the rest of the family heart attacks, and the business mogul is my older half-brother, Marcus."

"Fascinating," commented Isabella, her eyes intent. "One legend of a man who built an international company from nothing, his three very different wives and six children. When he died, his massive fortune was split nine ways between you…"

"Ten ways," interrupted Luke. "My oldest half-sister, Monica, is the only one of us who was married at the time of my father's death. A one-tenth share of the estate was placed in trust for her daughter, Megan."

"Monica would be the full sister of Marcus?" enquired Isabella, and Luke nodded.

"That's right, Monica and Marcus are the offspring from my father's first marriage to Celeste, I and my younger sister Susannah are from his second marriage, and Liam and my youngest half-sister Kristina are from his third marriage to Siobhan."

"Do you all keep in touch?" asked Isabella.

"They are my family," stressed Luke. "Maybe it is a complicated hotchpotch of steps and halves, but it's still my family, and I love them."

"Good." Isabella leant back in her chair, apparently satisfied. "I like you, Luke Blackwood, and I'm going to help you."

"What makes you think I need your help?" said Luke, amused.

"Well," drawled Isabella, fixing him with a beady gaze. "Given Arianna's aversion to rich men, add to that how she's going to feel when she finds out you've lied to her, and I'd say you're going to need all the help you can get."

"You're right," agreed Luke with a groan. "What do you suggest?"

"It's her birthday next week," Isabella informed him. "Here's what I propose we do," and Luke leant forward to listen…

~Chapter Eleven~
"Happy birthday, Mummy."

When Arianna finally came back into the garden, it was to find Luke and Isabella sipping wine and idly chatting about some play or other that Isabella had been to see the previous week and that Luke was thinking of seeing.

"Sorry it took me so long," she said, slipping back into her chair. "For some reason, Lucia insisted I read her practically the whole book."

Luke marvelled at the poker straight face Isabella kept as she sympathetically topped up Arianna's wine.

The next moment they jumped at a loud beep that emanated from Isabella's bag. She pulled out her mobile, quickly scanning the message with an impassive face, before dropping it back into her bag and turning apologetic eyes to them.

"Sorry Anna, it's work, I've got to go."

"Must you?" begged Arianna, then sighed with resignation. "Yes, I suppose you must."

"What do you do?" asked Luke, intrigued.

"Bella's an IT consultant," replied Arianna, and Luke heard the note of pride in her voice.

"She gets sent everywhere, sometimes all over the world, at a drop of a hat. Only, it is a bit of a nuisance when it interferes with dinner time."

"What can I say," shrugged Isabella, rising to her feet with a fluid, self-controlled grace which reminded Luke of a tiger about to spring. "It's work. It keeps bread on the table," and she swung her bag onto her shoulder.

Luke's eyes narrowed. He recognised the bag as a designer one his mother had long been coveting, her naturally frugal head warring frantically with her frivolous heart over its thousand-pound price tag.

He glanced curiously at Isabella, noting again the designer dress, and the handmade Italian shoes. Isabella's job, whatever it was, kept more than a humble loaf of bread on the table.

He said nothing, merely shook the hand she offered, agreed how nice it had been to meet her and that he hoped to meet her again, her expression not revealing by even the merest flicker the plans they'd discussed earlier.

Yes, Luke thought in admiration as Arianna went to see her out, Isabella Santorini was a force to be reckoned with, a woman he would avoid playing poker with, then Arianna walked back into the garden and at last, they were alone.

Luke swallowed, all thoughts of Isabella fleeing as she paused, looking steadily at him, eyes unsure and hesitant.

He held out a hand and she came to him, as he took her hand, he marvelled again at its smallness, at its apparent delicacy, knowing full well how hard those hands worked.

Gently, he pulled and tumbled her down onto his lap, groaning as his mouth closed over hers, feeling her eager need as her hands crept up into his hair, pulling him closer, her lips soft and yielding beneath his hungry desire.

For Luke, kissing had been merely a prelude to sex, a pleasant appetizer before the main course. Now, it was all that he wanted to do. Not that he didn't want her in every way possible, he did, of course, he did. But he sensed her shyness, knew she was inexperienced with men and had suffered at the hands of her husband.

Far from exasperating him, he found her naivety heart-wrenching. It aroused all his protective instincts. Knowing he could probably push her into going to bed with him made him not want to. It made him want to wait, take his time, let her set the pace and decide when the moment was right.

Maybe Marcus was correct, he thought wryly, maybe this was love.

Tenderly, he paid homage to her, gently kissing her forehead, her eyes, her cheeks, working his way down her throat, spending time in the sweet hollow he discovered there, lapping at it, delighting in her gasps and sighs.

This was so right, thought Luke, so right. This was the woman, the only woman.

Beyond rational consideration, beyond logic, beyond reasoning, Arianna's head fell backwards, gasping as Luke gently teased at her skin, his hands skimming down her arms, his body pressed to hers.

Never had she felt like this, so cherished, so worshipped, so adored. With Roberto, there had always been fear, apprehension, that if she didn't please him, he would be annoyed with her.

Not enjoying the sexual act, Arianna had learnt to pretend, to submit to him, anything to keep him happy and satisfied.

But now… She sensed Luke holding back, allowing her to set the pace, and she admired him for his restraint, for she could feel his need quivering in every pore of his body. To her total shock, she could feel her senses shivering in response. She wanted him back.

How could that be? Called frigid and sexless so many times by Roberto, Arianna had accepted it as the truth. She was frigid, inert, unattractive, and undesirable.

But now… Arianna felt herself unfolding to him like a flower to the sunlight. She knew she wanted him in every way a woman could want a man. Knew it was only a matter of time before they became lovers, and she trembled in anticipation. Shocked at herself that she could even contemplate becoming so intimate with a man she'd only just met, a man she barely knew.

The realisation hit with the force of a hurricane. It didn't matter. She loved him, no matter that it had only been a few days, no matter they barely knew one another, she loved him.

"Happy birthday, Mummy." Arianna blearily opened one eye as her bedside lamp was snapped on. She winced away from its brightness, mumbling, and attempted to burrow back down under the comfort of her duvet.

"Wake up, Mummy, it's your birthday! It's time to get up."

Groaning, Arianna reluctantly pulled herself up in the bed as Lucia danced up and down in an agony of excitement.

"Happy birthday!" she cried again. "I've brought you coffee," she continued and gestured towards the steaming cup of dark liquid on the bedside cabinet. Gratefully, Arianna sipped at it, feeling her body begin to awaken with every mouthful of the life-giving liquid.

"This is for you," Lucia declared, thrusting a small, pink box at her.

Arianna exclaimed with pleasure, carefully set down the cup and turned the box over in her hands, noting from the professionalism of the wrapping and extravagant organza bow that Lucia hadn't wrapped it herself.

"What a beautiful present," she said. "It seems almost a shame to open it."

"You have to!" cried Lucia in horror and bounced onto the bed.

"I said almost," Arianna reassured, holding up an arm for Lucia to crawl under. "Help me open it?" she asked. Eagerly, Lucia grasped one end of a ribbon and pulled, the whole lot neatly unfurling into a shimmering pile of pink.

Gently, Arianna eased aside the paper, and at the sight of the green jeweller's box, she turned startled eyes to Lucia's shiningly excited face.

"Open it, open it," urged Lucia.

With slightly trembling hands, Arianna slipped the catch and the box opened to reveal a beautiful pair of jade earrings.

"Lucia!" She stared at her daughter in shocked dismay, knowing they cost far more than Lucia could have had in her money box.

"How on earth did you afford these?"

"Don't you like them?" Lucia asked, her mouth quivering downwards. "I thought they matched your eyes. That's why I chose them."

"I love them," Arianna hastily reassured her. "They're so gorgeous, how could I not? But I'm worried about where you got the money from?"

"I emptied my moneybox," explained Lucia. "And Aunt Bella helped me with the rest." At the expression on her mother's face, she hurriedly added. "She said you'd be cross, so she put a note at the bottom of the box."

She fumbled the earrings out and handed her mother a small, neatly folded note.

"Anna," it read in Isabella's looping handwriting. "Please accept this gift in the spirit it is given and the love that is behind it. Please don't spoil the pleasure of giving for Lucia out of a mistaken sense of pride – and understand that sometimes money is not used to control – but is used to bring happiness to those we love."

Arianna dropped the note, her eyes brimming, and considered Lucia's hopeful expression. There was a long silence before she sighed, picked up the earrings and held them to her ears.

"Perhaps you'd better help me choose a dress to go with these," and felt a jolt of love at the relief and joy on her child's face.

Hustled out of the flat an hour later by a Lucia overflowing with importance at secrets being kept from her mother, Arianna found herself caught up in Lucia's excitement.

She tipped her head back to catch the sun's warming rays, thinking over the past week and wondering when she had ever been so happy.

She had seen Luke almost every day, each occasion tumbling her deeper and deeper in love until now a small sigh whispered past her lips, the very thought of him making her heart trip and her cheeks flush.

He was perfect; there was no other way to describe him. Mindful of Lucia, he took them all out on day trips, and instead of inviting Arianna out for dinner in the evening, had treated them both to lunch.

Seemingly happy to eat with the family in the evening at their small table, his eyes would meet Arianna's in an unspoken promise, never betraying – not even for an instant – that he was merely waiting for Lucia to go to bed so he could be alone with her mother.

Instead, he would patiently sit on the edge of Lucia's pink bed in her pretty, basement bedroom and read endless stories to her.

Clearing away the supper things, Arianna listened with a thrill of pleasure to his deep voice rumbling up the stairs. Then he would come upstairs to her, and the rest of the evening was theirs. At the thought of those evenings, Arianna felt herself go hot with delight.

Not lovers yet, their passion was becoming barely contained, and Arianna found herself desperately longing for more. She wanted to take his hand, take him into her bed and take what she was craving. Only the last lingering shreds of doubt, and the fact Lucia slept directly beneath her bedroom, delayed the inevitable.

They reached a local restaurant which specialised in brunches. Lucia pulled her through the door and there was Isabella, laughing at her surprise, guiding them to the table she had booked.

Arianna pushed away her plate, groaning at the thought of all the food she had eaten, and caught the excited look which Lucia shot at Isabella.

"What are you two smirking about?"

Isabella handed her an envelope.

"Happy birthday, Anna," she said. "This is your itinerary for the day, and there's to be no arguing. It's my gift to you."

Curiously, Arianna opened the envelope to find a neatly typed list, informing her that almost the whole afternoon was taken up by appointments with the beautician and hairdresser. Shocked, she looked at Isabella who was grinning widely.

"I can't accept this," she spluttered.

Isabella's grin deepened. "You can, and you will," she stated firmly.

Speechless, Arianna looked at the list to see that Luke was picking her up at seven for dinner and she was to dress smart-casual and pack an overnight bag.

"But … but …" she stuttered. "An overnight bag? I can't … What about Lucia?"

"Already sorted," reassured Isabella. "Lucia is spending the afternoon with me. We'll go home now and collect her things because she's going for a sleepover at Laura's house. I spoke to Laura's mother about it last week, and she says it's fine."

"Yes, it's all sorted," chimed in Lucia. "I'm going for a sleepover at Laura's, and you're going for a sleepover at Luke's," she added, in all innocence.

~Chapter Twelve~
"I want you to go now,"

Flame scorched Arianna's cheeks. She shot a hasty glance at Isabella, who raised her brows, the smile becoming suggestive, her eyes twinkling. Arianna took a deep breath.

Tonight, it was to be tonight. Good, screamed her body. At last, sighed her heart. She straightened in her chair. So be it.

"I see," she replied, looking at their beaming faces. "It's all sorted then, is it?"

They grinned and nodded.

"I suppose I should sit back, accept, and go with the flow," she murmured, and Lucia slipped off her chair to rush over and hug her mother.

"Happy birthday, Mummy," she squealed.

"Happy birthday, Anna," echoed Isabella, leaning forward and clasping Arianna's hand, a serious look on her face.

"You know," she said, "that may not be too bad a rule to stick to today. Sit back, accept, and go with the flow."

Hours later, Arianna leant back with a contented sigh, watching the hairdresser's assistant fuss around with a helmet contraption which apparently would steam the deep conditioning treatment even further into her hair.

Holding out her hands, she admired their creamy softness and the shimmering bronze gold nail polish which tipped each one, having to admit that so far, she had loved every single moment of Isabella's present.

The hairdressers being the last stop, now Arianna was looking forward to going home, leisurely packing herself a few things and finishing her preparations for seeing Luke, feeling a thrill of eager anticipation so intense it almost brought tears to her eyes.

"Now then," exclaimed Damien. Isabella's hairdresser, he had fitted Arianna in as a favour to Isabella – his favourite client – as he had proclaimed extravagantly.

"Let's see what we can do with this simply gorgeous hair," he stated, whipping out his scissors and comb.

Arianna watched in the mirror in fascination, observing the elegant, yet casual looking style which emerged from under his clever fingers, intently studying the way he blow-dried the curls under to create fullness and volume, and storing away the knowledge to try at home.

Damien had almost finished when the receptionist came to his side and whispered something in his ear. Damien frowned and put down the hairdryer.

"Will you excuse me for one minute, sweetie?" he begged, and Arianna nodded, watching as he went to the front desk and picked up the phone which was lying there.

Minutes ticked by and it became clear, that whatever the emergency was, it wasn't going to be solved quickly. Arianna eased her magazine back off the shelf, eager to continue with the rare treat of reading the latest issue of Cosmopolitan.

Finishing an article about a TV star who'd won her battle against cancer, Arianna glanced up, saw Damien still in brow-creasing discussion on the phone and happily turned to the next page.

Why Does Someone Deliberately Risk their Life? An in-depth interview with war photographer, Liam Blackwood.

Blackwood? What a coincidence, thought Arianna, and began to read, green eyes intense, as she learnt how the young man in question had always known he wanted to be a photojournalist.

How the assignments he hungered for had gradually become more dangerous, until finally, he ended up on the front line in Iraq, holding a camera with gunfire sounding all around him.

Bemused, Arianna shook her head, thinking although she admired him, she couldn't understand the need to risk all for a photograph.

She stared closely at the half-page picture of him. There was no doubt he was very good looking and those eyes...

Arianna frowned, what was it about those piercing blue eyes? They seemed familiar.

Leisurely, she turned the page, the interview now concentrated on Liam's personal life – what personal life, he laughed – the precious little free time he had was usually spent with his family.

His family, the interview went on, were, of course, the famous Blackwood family, one of the wealthiest families in the country. Arianna went cold all over, her heart thumping in her ear.

Opposite, stated the article, is a picture of Liam with his family after he received an award for outstanding bravery in the field of journalism.

Slowly, her eyes tracked across the page to the picture in question, knowing in advance what she would see.

Standing next to Liam, a hand clasped companionably on his shoulder, Luke gazed out into her shocked and disbelieving eyes.

"Sorry about that, sweetie."

Damien was back. Quickly, Arianna closed the magazine, sliding it silently onto the shelf, seeing her stunned reflection in the mirror.

"Celebrities," tutted Damien, drowning her mumbled reply in the hairdryer's roar.

Escaping the hairdressers – after plastering a fake smile on her face and reassuring Damien several times her hair was beautiful, amazing and she loved it – Arianna went to a newsagent's and bought the Cosmopolitan.

Resisting the urge to stand in the street and read it, she hurried home as fast as she could, where she read it again, over, and over in case she was wrong, or she'd been mistaken.

But no, it was true. Not only was Luke not as poor as he led her to believe – he was absolutely, stinking, rich – he was rolling in money.

He'd lied to her.

Arianna dropped the magazine to the ground, staring into space as her brain churned, refusing to believe it, thinking back over the past week, realising she had fallen in love with him and had allowed him further into her life, into her heart, than any other man had ever gone.

Not even Roberto had been trusted with her innermost soul the way Luke had. She buried her face in her hands with a groan. What a fool she had been. What a complete and utter fool.

But he was a man, so what had she expected?

Not only was he a man – he was a rich one to boot. Yet another wealthy arrogant bastard who imagined because he had money, he could control and manipulate.

After all, what on earth was she to him? A silly little nobody, somebody to amuse himself with and discard when he grew bored.

A growl rumbled in her throat and Arianna jumped to her feet, pacing angrily around the small flat. How dare he?

How dare he treat her this way!

Fuming, she stalked into the bedroom and ripped off the pretty dress she was wearing in honour of her birthday, pulling on her old, stained gardening shorts and t-shirt.

Storming into the garden and angrily dropping to her knees by the raised bed, she stabbed a trowel into the soft, brown earth, ferociously yanking out weeds and cutting back perennials.

Time passed and still, she drove her trowel into the ground, angrily swiping away tears with the back of her dirt-encrusted hand until finally it was seven and she heard the doorbell.

She paused and toyed with the idea of simply ignoring him, but her anger demanded more satisfaction than that.

Savagely, she threw down the trowel and stormed into the house, throwing open the front door to reveal Luke, handsome in silk shirt and beautifully cut trousers, his smile eager and welcoming behind a huge bouquet and a bottle of champagne.

"Happy birthday," he said, holding them out.

Wordlessly, she surveyed him, her face cold and unwelcoming, before turning and walking away from him into the flat.

Disconcerted, Luke closed the front door and followed, his brow creasing in a frown as she turned to confront him, and he took in her begrimed, bedraggled appearance.

"Sweetheart," he began. "I know I said smart-casual, but you seem to have veered a little too far into the casual…"

"I'm not coming," she stated flatly.

His eyes narrowed.

"What do you mean, you're not coming?"

"I mean, I'm not coming," she said, watching with satisfaction the flicker of alarm in his face.

"I see," he said, placing the bouquet and the champagne onto the table. "May I ask why?"

Arianna picked up the magazine folded to the article and tossed it to him. Instinctively he caught it, smoothing down the page.

He looked. Saw. Understood. His eyes shot up to hers, and now she saw panic in them.

"I can explain," he began.

"Can you?" Arianna's anger began to boil, brewing and bubbling. She faced him down, hands-on-hips, eyes spitting green fire.

"Can you really?"

"The shop *is* owned by my sister, Susannah," he said, desperation in his voice. "And it's true I offered to help while she was away on holiday. It's also true I work for ICRA, but … I own it. I was going to tell you in the restaurant that first evening. But then found out how much you were against rich men. I was worried if you found out I was wealthy you'd reject me without even giving yourself the chance to get to know me. So instead, I..."

"Lied to me," finished Arianna bluntly.

He winced.

"Not exactly lied," he insisted. "More, withheld the truth."

"A lie's a lie," she stated flatly. "But then, I wouldn't expect honesty from a wealthy man."

"What else was I supposed to do, Arianna?" he demanded. "You made it quite plain what your feelings were on the subject, completely black and white, no room for compromise or negotiation. This stupid prejudice you have..."

"Oh, so I'm stupid now, am I?" she snapped, and his face darkened.

"Of course, you're not stupid," he said. "Far from it, but your experience has left you with this bias. I was afraid you would be unable to see past it, to give us a chance, so I decided to wait, to let you get to know me. I was going to tell you tonight. I was going to take you to my apartment and tell you the truth."

"You expect me to believe that?" Arianna demanded, and Luke shook his head in despair.

"You can believe what you want, Arianna, it happens to be the truth."

She shook her head and he stepped towards her, taking her hand in his and pressing it to his chest. "Arianna," he began. "Please, don't do this to me, to us, please ... I love you..."

He said the words, those words. Up until a few hours ago, they were all she wanted to hear him say. Now, they left her cold, unmoved.

She stared at him, heartbreak in her eyes, and slowly, but determinedly, pulled her hand free and stepped away from him.

"I want you to go now," she said, her voice toneless and without emotion.

"Arianna…"

He tried to pull her to him, to hold her, make her see, understand … but she resisted. Pulled away. Her body was stiff and unresponsive.

"Arianna … please …" he begged in despair. "Don't do this. You and I have something here, something that could be amazing. Please don't throw that away. Please forgive me."

"No," she whispered. "Please … just go…"

He stared at her for the longest time, then she saw the weary acceptance on his face before he turned on his heel and left, slamming the door behind him.

She took the champagne into the kitchen and opened it, her face still and impassive as she tipped the foaming, bubbling contents down the sink and dropped the bottle in the bin.

The bouquet she also held over the bin, but the flowers were so beautiful, in the end, she didn't have the heart to destroy them.

Instead, she dumped them in a sink of water to deal with in the morning, then went into the garden and sat on a chair.

Numb, she felt numb.

She knew somewhere inside there were tears, but they were buried deep, locked away behind layers and layers of pain and anger.

Her throat constricted and she struggled to swallow past the large, heart-shaped obstruction lodged in it.

She sat, motionless and silent until it grew too dark to see, and then finally she went to bed.

~Chapter Thirteen~
"Your husband sends his regards,"

Next morning Arianna went to collect Lucia, her heart frozen, and her face stiff with unshed tears. During the night she came to the realisation it was all her fault.

She had trusted him, blindly and completely. She had been a fool and now she was being punished for it.

Learn from this, her furious head demanded of her grieving heart. Learn from this and never allow it to happen again.

Wearily she knocked on the door of Laura's house and Jess, her mother, opened it looking slightly surprised.

"Arianna," she exclaimed. "You're early. We weren't expecting you until at least lunchtime. Did you have a good time?"

"Yes, lovely, thank you," mumbled Arianna, feeling the tension in her face as she forced it to smile. "Is Lucia ready?"

"The girls went to the swings," replied Jess. Arianna knew she was talking about the small play area positioned a few yards down the road around the corner where Jess sometimes let them go and play. There were no roads to cross, it was a nice area, and both Jess and Arianna felt confident in their girls' ability to stay at the swings and not wander off.

"I'll go and get them," Jess began. "Let me get my shoes..."

"No, it's fine," insisted Arianna. "I'll go."

Quickly, she walked the few steps to the corner, noticing one of Jess's neighbours busy painting his garden fence – rhythm in his slow, steady brush strokes. She saw teenage boys sitting on a wall, all busy in their solitary world of texting, and heard the shouts and screams of children at play.

She stopped, realising the screams had taken on a desperate, terrified, edge. Her heart clutched with fear, and she began to run, sprinting around the corner to see her worst nightmare come true.

Lucia was struggling in the arms of a tall, muscular man who was dragging her from the swing. One mighty yank and he wrenched her from it with such force, the seat almost broke away from the chain. He carried her under his arm, kicking and screaming, and carried her towards a waiting black car.

Another man casually threw Laura, who was clawing at his arm, back across the playground. Arianna heard her cry and saw her trying to scramble back to her feet.

"Stop!" she screamed.

The men looked up, she saw their thuggish expressionless faces and ran faster than she ever thought possible, desperate to reach her child.

"Mummy!" yelled Lucia.

She saw the man holding her put something white over her mouth and nose, and Lucia went limp. Calmly, he threw her onto the backseat.

"Lucia! Let her go!" she screamed again.

Behind her, she heard the answering alarmed shouts of the youths. She reached him and was on him, kicking and punching, adrenalin giving her strength, frantic to get to her child whom she could see lying unconscious on the back seat of the car.

But the man was too strong for her. He brushed her off as easily as you would a fly, tossing her to the hard pavement with a grin of amusement.

"You won't take her!" she cried, scrambling back to her feet.

He turned from the car and ploughed his beefy fist into her face, sending her spinning once more to the ground, a shocked scream of pain ripped from her throat.

"Why?" she gasped, hands flying to her face, seeing the blood that poured.

"Your husband sends his regards," he sneered and jumped into the car, slamming the door as it took off in a screech of tyres, hotly pursued by the teenagers who chased it to the corner.

"Oh my god, do you want me to call the police?" Jess's neighbour stood there still clutching his brush, brown paint dripping onto his shoes. Behind him she saw Jess pelting down the road, eyes wide with shock.

"Give me that," Arianna shrieked, and snatched the paintbrush, shakily marking the registration number of the car on the pavement, hesitating when she reached the last letter.

"I can't remember," she cried in anguish. "Was it an N or an M, I can't remember, I can't remember!"

A hand took the paintbrush, and she looked up into the face of one of the boys.

"It was an M," he stated confidently.

She clutched at his arm. "Are you sure?"

He nodded, his eyes steady, and reached down and completed the registration.

Laura was crying, high thin wails of distress, as Jess enfolded her daughter in her arms.

"I tried to stop him, Mummy," she sobbed.

Arianna heard the neighbour explain in quick, tense words what had happened. Her eyes fixed on the empty swing still in motion as she fumbled in her bag for her phone.

With shaking hands, she dialled the one number she never thought she'd call again.

Marcus was at a loss. His plan to cheer his brother up after he arrived on his doorstep the previous evening, stony-faced, mouth a thin, grim line, explaining in a few terse words that Arianna had found out the truth and finished with him, seemed to get off to a flying start.

He took his taciturn brother to a bar and gradually wore him down in the time-honoured tradition with copious amounts of alcohol, which seemed to work, initially...

"Damn her!" Luke exploded belligerently. "I mean, I'm rich ... so what? What does she expect me to do, give all my money away? It won't change who I am, it won't change me, and it's clearly me she has the problem with."

He stared morosely into his beer as if expecting to find the answers there. At that point Marcus decided to take him home, pouring his beer-soaked brother into bed, and hoping things would seem better in the morning.

Now, Luke was surveying him beadily with bloodshot, accusing eyes over his coffee and Marcus felt a twinge of guilt.

"You'll get over her," he reassured him again. "Plenty more fish in the sea and all that…"

"I don't want a bloody fish," his brother snapped, then sighed. "I want her, and I've screwed it up, Marcus, royally and completely. She'll never trust me again."

"She'll come around," Marcus stated firmly. "You'll see. Give her a few days to miss you and she'll be phoning, hell, there's not a woman alive who can resist the Blackwood charm…" His voice trailed away at the look of utter despair on his brother's face.

"No," he said despondently. "You don't know her, Marcus, her pride, she'll never call me again, I've lost her…"

He paused, and the silence was filled with the ringing of his mobile. Both brothers' eyes automatically flicked to where it sat, Marcus raising a brow as Luke continued to ignore it.

"You going to get that?" he asked mildly.

"What's the point," Luke mumbled, reaching out a hand and picking it up. "It's probably either work or mum, neither of which I can … shit!" he exclaimed, looking at the caller ID. "It's her!"

He fumbled with the phone, nearly dropping it in his haste, and plastered it to his ear.

"Arianna, I … what?"

Marcus saw the confusion that crossed his brother's face; heard the high pitched, panicky voice on the phone; saw absolute horror crowd Luke's expression, which quickly changed into steely resolve.

"Go home, Arianna, I'm on my way. No, don't, I'll call the police, I have contacts, I'll be able to get this moving quicker. You did? Excellent, what is it?"

He snapped his fingers at Marcus, who instinctively thrust a pen and pad across the table towards him, watching in avid curiosity as Luke wrote down a registration number.

"Go home and I'll meet you there," his brother urged again, snapped off his mobile and looked at Marcus, eyes icy chips of flint, his chin firm.

Marcus stepped back from the cold hard resolve he saw on Luke's face.

"Luke," he gasped. "What the hell's happened?"

"That bastard Santorini's snatched Lucia…"

Pain. She thought she knew what that was. When her parents had both been taken from her in a plane crash mere weeks after she turned eighteen.

During the rapid disintegration of her marriage, its shameful conclusion, and the agonising discovery of what Roberto had done.

Last night, when she sat alone and heartbroken on her birthday, feeling her soul splinter over Luke's treachery.

She thought that was pain.

Now she knew, it hadn't even come close.

This was pain.

This wrenching and tearing; this trembling, blind, staring panic; this fear, this all-consuming, all-encompassing fear.

They'd taken her child.

She closed her eyes but there was no escape. Behind her lids, she saw Lucia's terrified face, saw the moment her little body went limp as she was thrown like a sack of dirty laundry into the car. She saw it drive away, taking with it her sole reason for existing.

"Lucia," she mumbled, through lips suddenly dry and cracked. "Oh baby, where are you, where's he taken you?"

She heard someone opening the door, looking up as Isabella let herself in with the key she possessed for emergencies, her eyes wide with alarmed concern.

"Arianna," she murmured, and Arianna turned to look at her. "Oh, your face!" she cried, then jumped as the doorbell sounded, hurtling down the hall to fling the front door open – flattening herself to the wall as Luke pushed past her - stopping in the entrance to the flat, his face hardening when he saw Arianna.

"Did the bastard do this?" he demanded. Arianna nodded and shook her head, confused.

A look flashed between Luke and Isabella.

"Tea, hot and sweet," he murmured, and Isabella quietly slipped into the kitchen.

"Not Roberto," she tried to clarify. "The man who took Lucia."

Luke frowned. "I thought Roberto took her?" he asked.

"No, he sent them."

Taking a deep breath, her grip on sanity slipping a little further, Arianna thrust away the blackness knowing it would in no way help Lucia if she fell apart.

Luke knelt before her, his gaze flicking over the rapidly darkening black eye, before settling on her, his expression confident and steady.

"Tell me," he ordered, so she did, everything from knocking on Jess's door to the moment she called him.

When she finished there was a second's silence as he digested the information, then he leant forward and gripped her arms.

"You must trust me, Arianna," he ordered, his eyes intensely blue. "We'll get her back. This is what I do, you must trust me, and you must believe we will get her back, I promise."

Arianna stared at him, then suddenly everything cleared in her brain, and she knew that in this at least, she did trust him, did believe he would do everything in his power to recover Lucia and would not rest until she was safely home again.

"I know," she said, quietly. "I trust you, Luke. Bring her back, please, bring her home."

~Chapter Fourteen~
"It's a small world, we will find them."

"Is there any news?" At his brother's quietly concerned question, Luke rubbed a hand over a face stiff with exhaustion and blinked eyes gritty through lack of sleep.

"Not yet," he admitted reluctantly. "We sent an agent to where he was living in Belize, but the house was closed up. When she questioned the staff, they told her the signor was away travelling and they didn't know when he'd be back."

Luke shook his head in despair. "He could be anywhere in the world, Marcus. The bastard had enough money to go anywhere, do anything."

Marcus nodded slowly, thinking back to that horrendous day two weeks ago when his brother roared out of his apartment, snapping orders into his phone as he left, talking directly to his contact at New Scotland Yard, instantly setting wheels in motion to find and apprehend the vehicle which had taken Lucia.

Unsurprisingly, the car had been reported stolen and was found the next day abandoned at a privately-owned airfield. By then it was obvious Lucia and her abductors had left the country.

Since that day, Luke had barely slept or stopped to eat, and Marcus watched in silent wonder as the vast, efficient, well-oiled machine that was ICRA swung into action.

A worldwide alert had been issued, and agents and informers across the globe were sent details and pictures of Lucia and Roberto.

Luke seemed constantly on the move, or the phone, personally checking and re-checking every lead – no matter how small or unlikely – the grim line between his eyes deepening with each false alarm.

"How's Arianna holding up?" Marcus asked.

Luke shook his head. "She's holding up for Lucia's sake," he confirmed, "but I'm worried if we don't get a break soon, she'll crack."

Marcus nodded again, thinking the same might well be true of his brother.

"Try to eat something, please Anna," Isabella begged, and Arianna numbly shook her head.

"I can't," she murmured. "I try, I do, but it chokes me." Isabella sighed in understanding, a frown pulling at her face as she anxiously surveyed her sister-in-law.

Always slight, now Arianna's clothes hung from a body which had shed pounds in the fortnight since it had happened. Isabella gently brushed a hand down her hollow cheek.

"I know," she replied. "But you need to eat. It won't help Lucia if you get sick. How about a cup of soup, something you don't need to chew?"

Arianna reluctantly nodded. Relieved, Isabella hurried to make it before she could change her mind, then stood over her, watching anxiously as Arianna slowly swallowed every drop.

"Feel better?" Isabella asked.

"Thank you."

Arianna managed a thin weak smile, then jolted almost out of her seat as the doorbell went.

"I'll go," said Isabella. She hurried to the door, her eyebrows shooting up at the sight of Luke, only to drop in disappointment as he grimly shook his head.

"How is she?" he murmured.

Isabella showed him the empty cup she still held. "She ate some soup," she replied.

Luke nodded, a flicker of satisfaction crossing his face, before following Isabella back into the flat to face Arianna and her hopeful, pleading eyes, knowing he would be forced to disappoint her yet again. One look at his face, and she knew.

"No leads at all?"

He shook his head. "I'm sorry," he said, guilt clawing at his throat. "I have every agent on it, I've called in every favour I'm owed by almost every police force in the world, every informant has been promised double money for any news of them, yet still nothing. It's as if they've vanished into thin air." He broke off at the despair on Arianna's face, cursing his stupidity.

"We will find them," he desperately reassured her. "It's a small world, we will find them."

"But what's happening to my baby in the meantime?" Arianna demanded. "She must be so scared and confused. She thought her father was dead. Now this man is telling her he is her father. Bella, you were right, I should have told her ages ago, at least she'd have been prepared!"

"It's not your fault," Isabella insisted, rushing to Arianna's side. "How could you have ever known he'd do something like this? You did what you thought was right, so don't blame yourself."

Reluctantly, Arianna nodded, and Isabella gave her a reassuring hug. "Why don't you have a nap?" she suggested, and lead Arianna unresisting into the bedroom.

When she returned, Luke had gone into the garden and Isabella followed him out, relieved to have a chance to talk privately with him.

"Why now?" she demanded bluntly, and Luke blinked, startled by her question. "Why now?" she continued. "He's been gone seven years, why leave it this long to take Lucia? If he wanted his child, why not take her with him when he left? Or, if it wasn't possible, why has he waited so long to abduct her?"

"I don't know," Luke slowly shook his head. "I did wonder that myself, but couldn't..."

"What has changed in Arianna's life?" Isabella interrupted fiercely. "For seven years things have jogged along, then suddenly in less than a fortnight, two monumental changes occur in her life, Lucia is snatched and before that..."

"She met me..." Luke finished, turning horrified eyes onto Isabella. "Are you saying it's my fault? That because Arianna and I... that's why he...? But why, Isabella? He left them without a backwards glance, there's been no communication between them, so why would he care if Arianna started seeing someone?"

"You don't understand the kind of a man he is," replied Isabella, eyes narrowing with disdain.

Luke pulled out a garden chair and motioned her to it. "Tell me," he insisted.

Isabella sat, waiting until he was seated at the table before continuing.

"Supremely arrogant," she began. "Completely self-focused, unable to comprehend that other people could have emotions and motives different from their own." Isabella tapped her short, blunt nails on the wooden table, her eyes thoughtful as she focused on the past.

"When he left, he had no idea Arianna was on the verge of taking Lucia and running. His arrogance would never have allowed him to even consider the possibility of his wife disobeying him in such a way." She leaned across the table, her eyes never leaving Luke's face as she tried to make him understand.

"All the years he's been gone he was happy to leave Arianna and Lucia here, kept on ice, waiting until he was ready. Then he would have snapped his fingers and expected them to come running, his faithful, patient wife, a ready-made family his for the taking."

She looked steadily at Luke.

"Then she met you," she continued. "And suddenly, everything changed."

"But that would mean, he's been having her watched all this time," Luke stated.

Isabella nodded in agreement.

"It's the only explanation," she said. "The only one I can make fit anyway." She watched Luke take on board all she had said, saw him reluctantly, guiltily, agree with her.

"So," he began slowly. "If that's true, what do you think...?"

"Luke!"

At Arianna's urgent shout Luke shot from the chair and rushed back into the house, closely followed by Isabella, to find Arianna standing at the bedroom door, her mobile clutched to her ear, a wild look of panic on her face.

"I can't understand what he's saying," she cried. "He said my name and Lucia's and started talking in some language I can't understand!"

Quickly, Luke snatched the phone.

"Yes?" he barked. He listened to the garbled torrent of words, and then answered in a language that Isabella recognised as Portuguese.

The conversation went on, the women unconsciously clutching at each other, watching as Luke's expression changed from suspicion to cautious hope, to relief, then to resolution.

He began to relay what was obviously a set of instructions, grabbing the pen and notepad from the table and hurriedly scribbling down an address. Finally, he hung up and looked at them.

"We've found her," he stated, and Isabella supported Arianna as her legs buckled.

"Where? How?" she gasped.

"Brazil," Luke grinned, picking Arianna up and holding her tightly. "That was a very honest and concerned farmer from a remote province. About a week ago his ten-year-old daughter came home with what he thought was a wild tale of a beautiful little princess who was being held captive in a deserted house high up in the hills."

Arianna pulled away from his grasp, her face taut with concern at the tale he was telling.

"At first dismissive, he then became concerned when his daughter went to play every day with this little girl, telling her father she had found a hole in the fence, but she had to be careful as there were mean men with guns who guarded the princess." At Luke's words, Arianna paled, clutching at him in fear.

"Yesterday, he made his daughter take him to meet the princess. Sure enough, there was a gap in the fence, too small for him to go through but large enough for his daughter to squeeze into the garden and bring the princess to meet her father. She told him her name was Lucia."

A dry sob was wrenched from Arianna's throat at the mention of her child's name.

"He only speaks a few words of English but understood enough to learn the princess had been taken away from her mother and was being held against her will. He's a kind, soft-hearted father and promised to help her, so made the long trip into the nearest town to telephone you."

"But how did he know my number?" gasped Arianna, and Luke smiled.

"Lucia still had her piece of paper with it written on in her pocket. She gave it to him. He knew she was English, so he was able to find out the right international code to use."

"Oh," exclaimed Arianna, clutching her hand to her mouth, tears of relief spurting from her eyes. "Oh, Thank heavens," she muttered. "What happens now?" she demanded.

"Now, I go and get her," replied Luke grimly, and Arianna nodded, her eyes shining.

"Thank you," she said quietly.

"Can I do anything to help?" Isabella asked.

"Well, it would be useful if you could get hold of an unlicensed private jet to get us to Brazil and back without leaving a paper trail," Luke drawled. "Because if you could, it would save an awful lot of time going through official channels."

Isabella's eyes narrowed. Turning on her heel she stalked from the house, pulling her phone from her bag. Luke's jaw dropped and he made to go after her but was pulled back by Arianna calling his name.

"I'm going with you," she announced firmly.

Luke shook his head. "No, you're not."

Arianna's chin rose. "She's my child," she snapped. "I want to be there. I have to be."

"No, Arianna," he said again. "It'll be dangerous. If I'm having to worry about you, it could compromise the operation and put Lucia's life in danger."

There was a long silence. Luke saw conflicting emotions warring across Arianna's face before she finally sighed and reluctantly nodded.

"I understand," she said. "I wouldn't want to endanger you or Lucia in any way, but please, be careful, and please, bring my baby home."

"I will," he promised.

He left swiftly, striding down the street back to his car, his whole body tight with anticipation.

"Luke!" He turned as Isabella hurried up and thrust a small square of paper into his hands. "Be at this airfield at 16:00 hours," she ordered. "A plane will be waiting for you, fully fuelled and ready to fly you to wherever you need to go."

Luke took the paper in stunned surprise, staring first at it and then at Isabella.

"Who are you?" he breathed.

Isabella smiled – a dangerous smile that didn't quite reach her eyes. "I told you," she said. "I'm Isabella Santorini, an IT consultant and Arianna's friend. That's all you need to know." Silently, Luke surveyed her, nodded, and tucked the paper into his pocket. "Oh, and Luke..."

"Yes?"

"Don't ask the pilots any questions otherwise they will not hesitate to kill you and throw your body out of the plane."

~Chapter Fifteen~
"You go now,"

The plane was small, sleek, and silent. As Luke gazed mutely around in admiration, he reflected on the frenzied few hours of activity which lay behind him.

Getting together a few essentials, he asked for a volunteer to go with him. Proud when every field agent not currently assigned had stepped forward and offered.

He chose Sullivan, a giant of a man in his early thirties. A colleague and a close friend of Luke's for several years, James Sullivan was a good guy to have by your side in a tricky situation. Moreover, knew how to keep his mouth shut and his thoughts to himself.

Bearing in mind Isabella's bizarre warning, Luke figured this to be an advantage on this mission.

Upon reaching the airfield a woman had greeted them, her slim hips clad in army issue green, long blonde hair scraped brutally back from chiselled cheekbones, her eyes chips of blue ice.

Beside him, Luke sensed Sullivan's air of interest, but if the blonde had also seen it, she chose to ignore it, instead turning that steely gaze onto Luke.

"Blackwood?" she snapped, and Luke nodded. "Follow me," she ordered, swung on her heels, and led the way over the small runway to where a plane awaited them, its dark, reflective surface bouncing the late afternoon sunlight into their eyes.

"This is Piers," she announced, stopping where a small, neat man of Asian extract was leaning against the plane having a cigarette.

"He will be your pilot," the blonde continued, and her gaze hardened.

"He doesn't speak much English, so don't waste your time attempting to engage him in conversation. He knows what is to be done. When you reach your destination, he will land at a private airfield fifteen kilometres from the house where the girl is being held. A jeep will be available for your use."

Luke nodded, thankful for the precise arrangements, again wondering precisely *who*, or rather *what*, Isabella Santorini was to be able to call in such monumental favours.

"You will have a four-hour window," the blonde informed him. "After that, the plane will return to the UK – with, or without you – Mr Blackwood," her tone indicating it was of supreme indifference to her either way.

"Thank you," Luke began, but the blonde had already turned and was stalking back across the tarmac, her ramrod straight spine and long, efficient stride screaming of military training.

The men watched her go, a shared second of mutual male admiration evident in the looks

Luke and Sullivan exchanged, and the gleam Luke was sure he spotted in the pilot's eyes.

The man stubbed out his cigarette and jerked a thumb at the plane.

"We go now," he ordered in broken, heavily accented English. Hastily, Luke and Sullivan shouldered their packs and complied.

Soon, the two men were buckled into comfortable seats waiting for take-off from an unlisted airfield, which Luke had not previously known the existence of, in a state-of-the-art plane, which Luke assumed wouldn't be registered anywhere either.

Sullivan's hand briefly brushed Luke's shoulder. He jerked his head forward and Luke watched in narrow-eyed silence as a second pilot climbed aboard.

Dressed in unrelieved black the same as Piers, this pilot also wore an all-concealing balaclava over his face.

"What do you suppose...?" Luke quietly murmured.

Sullivan shrugged. "Someone high profile enough we'd recognise him?" he queried under his breath.

Luke shook his head, watching as the pilot entered the cockpit, the door firmly closing behind him.

It was a long trip.

The men filled in the time going over the scant information they had hastily acquired. Satellite shots of the area, a map showing the roads in and out, a rough sketch of the house provided by the farmer, whom Luke had phoned back as arranged and spoken to at length, telling the man to keep his daughter away from the house.

He didn't want any civilians to be in the way, especially if she was correct and there were mean men with guns guarding the princess.

At the thought of Lucia being scared and alone, Luke's jaw tightened, and he glanced at the packs where their weapons were stored.

That bastard Santorini and his hired thugs would soon find even meaner men, with even bigger guns, were on their way.

Finally, Luke felt his eyelids grow heavy and he lay back in the chair letting sleep wash over him, thinking it would be a good idea to get some rest while he could.

He jerked awake what felt like mere moments later, but could have been hours, as the plane banked sharply sideways and he instinctively braced himself, glancing around at Sullivan.

"What's happening?"

Sullivan paused in his job of tucking all his dreadlocks under a black, woollen hat.

"Think we're here," he said and flashed him a grin, perfect white teeth gleaming against his caramel-coloured skin.

He continued pulling together his gear, eyes taking on an intense sheen which Luke knew meant his mind was already completely focused on the task ahead.

Silently, the two men waited as the plane taxied to a gentle stop, watching as the second pilot left the cockpit. He opened the plane's doorway, let down the steps, and vanished down them into the dark South American night.

"Where do you suppose he's going to in such a hurry?" Sullivan enquired mildly, under cover of standing and swinging his gear onto his back.

"I have no idea," Luke replied. "But it's probably best if we don't ask."

Piers also left the cockpit and beckoned to them. The two men followed him down the steps and out onto the tarmac. He pointed to a sturdy, dark jeep waiting at the edge of the runway.

"You go now," he said, then pointed to his wristwatch and held up four fingers.

"Yeah, yeah, we know," reassured Luke, dryly. "You'll hold the bus for four hours, and if we're not back by then you'll go home without us."

The little man's face split into a grin, he clapped them both on the shoulder and held up fingers crossed for luck.

"You go now," he said again, clambering back into the plane, pulling the steps up behind him and snapping the door closed.

Luke glanced at Sullivan, who shrugged, his rugged face showing amusement.

"Guess we'd better go now," he said.

They walked quickly to the jeep, threw their gear in, and swung into the seats, Luke taking the wheel whilst Sullivan tried to make sense of the map.

Luke sped over the uneven mud track. Mindful of the clock ticking he increased his speed, Sullivan cursing as the jeep jounced in a deep pothole throwing the men up roughly in their seats.

Finally, they reached the rendezvous point. Luke stopped, killing the engine, and flashed the headlights, once, twice, a long pause, then once again.

There was a moment, then a torch flashed, once, twice.

A man stepped from the darkness, swarthy, heavyset, dressed in simple working clothes. He walked towards them, a large slender hound trotting by his side.

Its eyes rolled at the sight of them, a growl sounding low in its throat until the man raised his hand and spoke to it, low and reassuring. Instantly, the dog sat, its gaze fixed unswervingly on its master.

"Senhor Blackwood?" he asked hesitantly, and Luke answered him in rapid Portuguese.

"Yes, thank you for meeting with us. Where is the house where Lucia is being held?"

The man gestured into the darkness behind him, then saw the map in Sullivan's hand and leaned over it.

Frowning, he took the pencil Sullivan pulled from his pocket and drew with hands that only slightly shook a roughly oblong shape on the map, sketching in a line from the track they were on to it, explaining how an old forgotten path led from the track to the house.

"Where is the gap in the fence?" asked Luke. The man drew a perimeter around the oblong and marked a small x halfway down one side of it.

"It is the best place to go in," he said. "It is sheltered behind bushes and trees. It is how my daughter was able to escape detection. You will need my dog," he suddenly stated, gesturing to where the dog still sat.

"That's very kind of you," replied Luke, slightly taken aback. "But I don't think…"

"The house is guarded at night by a pair of the most vicious dogs," the farmer continued.

"We can't risk the noise of a dogfight," Luke stated. "And besides, one against two…"

"She is female," the farmer explained patiently in English. "And it is time for her to make puppies…"

He raised his eyebrows meaningfully at the two men, and Luke wondered at the simple brilliance of the plan.

"Thank you," he said.

The man clicked his fingers at the dog, gesturing towards the back of the jeep. Instantly, she sprang inside and sat, panting hot breath all over the back of Luke's neck.

"Thank you, Senhor," said Luke again, and shook the man's hand. "Thank you for all your help. Now go home and make sure your daughter stays safely in her bed tonight."

"I will," reassured the man, and turned to go, then stopped and looked at Luke seriously.

"Please, Senhor Blackwood, will you let me know when the princess has been rescued. My daughter, she is very worried about her. It would be good to be able to put her mind at rest."

"Of course," reassured Luke.

The man nodded and stepped away from the jeep, the velvety darkness of the night swallowing him whole.

"Nice guy," observed Sullivan. "Lot of people wouldn't have put themselves at risk, not even for a child."

"He's a father himself," replied Luke. "I guess he imagined how he would feel if it was his daughter who'd been kidnapped."

He started the jeep again and drove steadily into the darkness, keeping his eyes peeled for the markers which the farmer had described to them

– the twisted tree, the boulder that looked like an ear, and finally, a group of small, stunted thorn bushes which marked the beginning of the trail.

Quickly, Luke reversed the jeep into the shadow cast by the bushes and the two men got out, shouldering their packs easily.

"What about her?" Sullivan asked, gesturing to the dog still sitting patiently in the jeep, pink tongue lolling as she stared casually back.

"Come," said Luke in Portuguese.

Obediently, the dog leapt from the vehicle and trotted over to them, her wet nose briefly pushing into his hand.

They cast around until they found the rough track, thankful for the full moon which kept the need for torches to a minimum.

Silently, they walked for almost five minutes until Luke held up a hand and pointed. Beside him, Sullivan looked and nodded. They crept stealthily forwards, aiming for the light which could now be seen ahead.

Finally, they reached a tall wire fence, feeling their way cautiously along until they located the gap the farmer had spoken of. Pulling wire cutters from his pack, Sullivan snipped at the strands until a hole big enough to take a man was created.

Quietly, they slipped through, emerging into the grounds behind a group of low bushes, carefully pushing their way through until they were crouched in the shadows on the very edge, the dog still and silent beside them.

~Chapter Sixteen~
"But he's going to kill you."

Luke glanced up. The moon was about to sail behind a large, dark cloud. He touched Sullivan on the shoulder, pointing upwards. His colleague nodded in understanding.

They patiently waited.

At last, the cloud pulled itself protectively across the face of the moon plunging everything into total darkness, then they ran, crouching low, keeping a wary eye out for guards, human or canine until they reached the looming cover of the house and flattened themselves against it.

Sullivan pulled out his housebreaking kit and set about picking the brand-new window lock, whilst Luke kept watch, his weapon cold and reassuring in his steady hands.

A low growl rumbled in the silence.

He looked up, heart leaping with adrenalin. A dark shape trotted around the side of the house, quickly followed by another.

Beside him, Luke felt the farmer's dog quiver with interest.

Bending low, he whispered 'go' in Portuguese in her ear, and she fled like a rocket past the two male dogs.

Luke could have sworn he saw their noses twitch as the ripe, rich scent of a female desperate to be mounted, shot past them.

They chased after her, dismissing their duties without a second thought, caught up in the primitive urge to mate.

Sullivan expertly finished with the lock and stealthily pushed the window open. Luke held his breath. There'd been no time to determine if the house were alarmed, so he prayed Santorini assumed its remote location, plus guards, would be enough to keep the world at bay.

The house remained silent. Quickly, they climbed inside and found themselves in what looked to be a study. Gently, Luke eased the door open, peering into the dimly lit hall beyond.

The farmer told him Lucia said her room was at the back of the house on the second floor, and Luke hoped this was correct, not fancying the idea of searching the whole, vast house.

It was late, gone midnight. Luke was counting on the household being in bed, still, they walked quietly, merging effortlessly into the shadows, easing their way down the hall and up the stairs, one flight, two until finally, they were at the very top of the house.

A wide passageway stretched the length of the house with a row of six doors leading to rooms at the back of the house.

Luke motioned Sullivan to go to the other end and start checking, whilst he turned to the door nearest him.

Listening at its thick, wooden surface, he heard nothing, then gently squeezed the door handle around and opened the door, peering into a large empty room devoid of any furniture except a few storage crates piled haphazardly in one corner.

The next room was also empty, although this one did contain a few articles of bedroom furniture. Luke could tell from the clothes thrown onto the bed that a man used this room and wondered if it belonged to one of the guards.

The next door had been painted white. In a sudden shaft of moonlight, Luke could see a small design of pink flowers painted on it.

Certainty clutched him that this was the room. Softly, quietly, he eased the door open and slipped inside.

The room was dimly lit by a pretty, pink lamp. Looking around, Luke saw a white canopied bed; pretty, little girl furniture; rows of books pristine in their newness; and what looked like every toy known to man, or rather child, sitting neat and untouched on white painted shelves.

He glanced instinctively at the bed.

It was empty.

Panicked, he looked wildly around and saw a small, pyjama-clad figure huddled on the window seat looking out at the night, her back to the room.

"Miss?" he murmured, not wishing to alarm her.

Lucia's back stiffened.

"I told you," she stated, her voice imperious, and Luke grinned with amused pride that her spirit was unbroken and her will unbowed.

"I'm not hungry and I won't eat it, whatever it is you've brought this time, so take it away and."

She swung around, her eyes nearly popping out of her skull when she saw him.

"Luke!" she squeaked.

Hurriedly Luke shushed her.

"I knew you'd come for me," she whispered and hurled herself into his arms.

Instinctively, Luke's arms closed around her. Hugging the small form clinging desperately to his neck, his heart cracked, and he realised as much as he loved the mother, so did he love the child.

Finally, he pulled away and looked at her.

"Are you all right?" he asked, and she nodded, her eyes wide and solemn.

"Get some shoes and warm clothes on," he ordered crisply. "We're getting out of here."

Lucia swallowed, then rushed to do his bidding, pulling a jumper over her head, and stuffing her feet into trainers.

She stopped and stared at him. Her small face was serious.

"I knew you'd come for me," she said again. "I knew it. When he ... that man, my father, said no one would ever find me, I knew he was lying, I knew you would."

"I wouldn't have known where to look," Luke told her. "That was a very brave and clever thing you did, giving your mother's phone number to that girl." She nodded again, biting her lip.

On an impulse, Luke dropped to his knees and enfolded her in his arms again, feeling her shake with suppressed fear.

"Come on honey," he said quietly. "Let's go home."

He rose and turned, her hand in his, and his heart stopped at the sight of the man who now lounged in the doorway.

His cruelly handsome face – a twisted male mockery of Isabella's – was split by a contemptuous grin and the small automatic in his hand was aimed directly at Luke's chest.

Time stood still. Luke stared into Roberto Santorini's eyes, saw what resided there, and knew this man wouldn't hesitate to kill him.

Where the hell was Sullivan, he thought desperately, brain racing as he considered and dismissed tactics and strategies.

Lucia's hand – warm and clammy with fear – was grasping tightly onto his. Gently he tried to ease it free, needing to get her out of the line of fire, but her grip tightened.

"Blackwood," Santorini hissed the name, his eyes narrowing with displeasure. "How did you find us?"

"Does it matter?" demanded Luke and Santorini shrugged carelessly.

"Not really," he agreed. "Considering that you're going to die here."

"You can't do that!" Lucia gasped.

Santorini smiled; a thin, cruel smile that didn't reach his eyes.

"My dear child," he drawled. "I will do whatever it takes to keep you safe, and this man must be eliminated. Now, step away from him."

"No," insisted Lucia, gripping Luke's hand with surprising strength.

"Lucia, you will do as you are told," demanded Santorini, and Lucia stuck her tongue out at him in such a childish display of bravado that Luke wanted to laugh out loud.

"Shan't!" she yelled.

Luke saw displeasure wash over Santorini's face.

"Lucia." Luke looked down at her and gently stroked her cheek. "Everything will be ok, but I need you to go and sit on the bed. I don't want you to get hurt."

"But he's going to kill you." Tears spurted from Lucia's eyes, and she scrubbed furiously at them with the back of her hand.

"I'll be fine," Luke reassured her.

Reluctantly, slowly, Lucia released his hand and moved toward the bed.

"How very touching," sneered Santorini. "But unfortunately, she's right. I am going to kill you."

He raised his gun and fired at point-blank range, but Luke had been anticipating this.

In the split second before Santorini squeezed the trigger, he was already moving, leaping backwards, deliberately sending the lamp flying, plunging the room into pitch darkness.

The gun roared.

With a pounding heart, Luke heard Lucia scream, but couldn't call out to her for fear of giving his position away to Santorini.

Knowing he would be expecting Luke to rush him, Luke threw himself as far right as he could, hit the ground and rolled, his wound ripping open as his powerful legs punched out in a scissor movement, knocking Santorini violently to the floor.

Once again, the gun shouted in the dark as Santorini aimed and fired in the direction of the attack.

But Luke was already not there.

His mind, white-hot and focused, his body running on adrenalin, refused to let him feel the agonising pain in his side.

He rolled and kicked in the darkness, praying he had judged right, feeling a jolt of triumph as his feet found their target and Santorini howled in pain and anger, hitting the floor with an almighty crash.

Rearing up like an avenging angel, Luke's mighty fists clasped together, and he punched downwards, feeling the satisfying thud as they met flesh and he heard Santorini's body slump to the ground.

Then, there was silence.

Cautiously, Luke moved silently and swiftly away, concerned that perhaps he had only winded him, and even more concerned he might still have the gun.

There was the sound of running feet outside and Luke braced himself to face the guards. The door was suddenly and violently kicked open.

Luke blinked at the blinding light pouring in from the landing. Seeing no one there, he waited, crouching in the darkness.

"Luke?"

At Sullivan's low, concerned voice, Luke relaxed.

"In here," he confirmed. "I think Santorini's down but be careful."

A hand snaked around the corner and flipped on the light. Luke hurriedly looked down to see Santorini lying unconscious on the floor, a dark, livid bruise already purpling his cheek. Luke nodded, satisfied.

"That one's for Arianna," he muttered under his breath. "He's down," he assured Sullivan, and the large man slipped into the room closing the door behind him.

Luke looked around wildly for Lucia, seeing only an empty room.

"Lucia?" he hissed in panic and was rewarded by a scared little voice from under the bed.

"Luke?"

There was a scuffle and a pair of trainer-clad feet emerged, quickly followed by the rest of her as Lucia wiggled out and threw herself into his arms.

"I was so scared," she whispered. "I thought he'd killed you." She looked down at the prone body of her father, her lip curled back in distaste.

"Is he dead?" she asked curiously, looking almost disappointed when Luke shook his head.

"No, unconscious," he replied and looked up at Sullivan. "Where the hell were you?" he demanded.

Sullivan rubbed ruefully at his swollen jaw. "Ran into a little trouble myself," he confided. "Couple of Santorini's goons thought they could take me out."

"Where are they now?" Luke asked.

White teeth flashed as a wry grin spread across Sullivan's face.

"Having a little nap," he drawled, and Luke felt an answering smile tug at his lips.

"Come on, honey." He turned back to Lucia. "We have to get out of here."

~Chapter Seventeen~
"You're home."

Luke stood up and went to lift Lucia, wincing as he finally registered the excruciating pain in his side. Putting a hand to it, it came away all bloody and Lucia's eyes went wide.

"You've been shot!" she gasped, and Luke shook his head.

"No, it's an old wound," he reassured her, pushing her towards Sullivan.

"You go," he ordered. "Take Lucia and wait for me at the jeep, I'll make sure Santorini can't raise the alarm."

Sullivan nodded, but Lucia, eyes wide in terror at the huge, intimidating man, clung to Luke's hand, burrowing herself into his side.

"No," she whimpered. "I want to stay with you." Luke knelt by her side.

"Sweetie," he comforted her. "I know you're scared, and I understand you don't know Sullivan, and he does look kind of scary, but do you know, I've seen him shaking in his boots because his mum yelled at him…"

"Hey," protested Sullivan.

Luke raised his brows at him in amusement. A hulk of a man, Luke had seen Sullivan take out armed kidnappers with one kick of his powerful legs, but quail in terror at his mother's displeasure. A tiny, hothead of a woman born in London's East End, she ruled her easy-going Jamaican husband and raised her son to be respectful and courteous to all women.

"Really?" Lucia surveyed Sullivan in interest. "What did you do? Were you very naughty?"

"Oh, yeah," Sullivan shook his head. "I'd been real naughty."

"I'm naughty as well, sometimes," confided Lucia, her grip on Luke's hand loosening as she stepped towards Sullivan. "But my mummy doesn't yell, she gets all sad and looks at me."

"Oh, man," sympathised Sullivan, and held out his hand. "You get the look? I guess that's even worse than the yelling." Lucia nodded and took his hand confidently.

"Now, sugar," said Sullivan seriously. "You've got to stay quiet and do exactly what I tell you, reckon you can do that?"

Lucia nodded importantly.

"But what about Luke?" she asked.

"I'll be right behind you, I promise," he reassured her, then looked at Sullivan. It was a look that clearly said go, and don't wait too long for me. Sullivan nodded, then cautiously creaked the door open, peered into the corridor outside and eased from the room, taking Lucia with him.

Luke turned back to the task at hand, looking for some rope or tape, anything to immobilise Santorini.

A skipping rope folded neatly on one of the shelves served the purpose of securing his prone body tightly. Luke found a bright, pink, gauzy scarf tied around the neck of a large doll and took great delight in gagging Santorini with it.

Stepping back, he surveyed his handiwork with satisfaction, then froze at the quiet click behind him, and the low, heavily accented Portuguese voice.

"One wrong move, Blackwood, and I shoot. Now put your hands where I can see them and turn around, nice and slowly."

Cursing himself for being so careless, Luke slowly raised his hands and turned, to find a short, bald man all dressed in black, aiming an automatic at his head.

The man's eyes flicked to Santorini, then back to Luke. "I assume, as you've gone to all the effort of securing him, he's not dead?" He paused, a look of disdain crossing his face.

"That was a mistake, Blackwood. If you'd killed him, you would have been long gone, but your weakness will be your downfall as I have no such scruples." He raised his gun.

Once again, Luke stared into the face of death.

Suddenly, a dark figure appeared in the doorway behind the man. Luke gaped in shock as the newcomer aimed a lethal kick at the bald man which sent him stumbling forward, the gun flying from his hand.

Luke stepped back as the dark figure, whom he saw to his surprise was the second pilot from the plane, efficiently gripped the bald man's arm, and twisted it sharply back into an unnatural angle. Luke heard the crack of breaking bone and the man's demented howl of pain.

The pilot aimed a sharp, chopping blow to the back of the man's skull which crumpled him soundlessly to the ground, then knelt beside his prone body. He looked up, surprisingly dark eyes glinting through the slits of his balaclava.

"Go!" ordered the pilot, in low, gruff French. When Luke hesitated, he picked up the gun and pointed it unswervingly at him.

"Go!" he ordered again.

Luke did as he was told, rushing from the room, and silently hurrying down the stairs, frowning at the blood beginning to gush from his wound. Without breaking his stride – he ripped the sleeve from his shirt and balled it against his side – gritting his teeth against the pain.

Quickly, he ran from the house. Seeing no sign of either the guard dogs or the farmer's dog, he hoped she somehow found her way safely home to her master. Then he was at the gap in the fence and wiggled through, pelting along the track as fast as he could, mindful of time ticking by and a plane that would not wait.

Sullivan had already reversed the jeep out onto the track and was waiting, engine silently running, a grim expression on his face. Luke burst from the shrubs and hurled himself breathlessly into the jeep, and Sullivan took off in a cloud of dust and a screech of tyres.

Leaning back with a groan, happy to let Sullivan take the wheel for the return journey, Luke glanced over his shoulder at Lucia huddled on the narrow seat behind him, her face a tight mask of mixed fear and relief.

He flashed her a quick, comforting smile in the moonlight, which she bravely tried to return, but her mouth quivered downwards. Luke realised she was almost at the end of her tether and reached back to pat her shoulder reassuringly.

Within minutes it seemed they were roaring up to the airfield, where Piers was waiting anxiously by the plane, his face splitting into a grin of relief when he saw them.

As they hurried past him up the steps, his hand rested gently on Lucia's head and he nodded at Luke, conveying his pleasure that they had been successful.

Settling Lucia into a seat, Luke watched as Piers hurried on board, wondering about the other pilot, concerned whether the man who'd saved his life had got away safely and if maybe he should try and get Piers to hold the plane.

Sullivan pulled off his hat, and Lucia stared in wonder at his dreadlocks. Kneeling up in her seat, she reached out a hand to pat them.

"How do you brush your hair?" she asked.

Sullivan grinned. "That's the beauty of them, sugar. I don't have to."

Lucia sank back into her seat, a speculative gleam entering her eyes and Luke felt a twinge of amusement at the thought of her demanding her hair be put into dreadlocks and Arianna's reaction to it. Taking down a blanket from the overhead locker, he snuggled it around Lucia.

"Try to get some sleep," he advised. "It's a long flight home." Lucia, her eyes sleepy, nodded.

Luke glanced out the window, as a jeep roared onto the airfield with the familiar slight figure of the second pilot at the wheel, pleased the other man, whoever he was, had made it. Moments later there was a thud as if something had been loaded into the cargo hatch behind, and then the second pilot was clambering aboard, pulling up the stairs behind him.

He paused, raised a hand at Luke, who returned the gesture, and then disappeared into the cockpit, once more shutting the door firmly between the pilots and the watching men.

"What was that all about?" Sullivan muttered in interest.

Quietly, so as not to wake the already sleeping Lucia, Luke told him what had happened. Sullivan nodded slowly, then frowned as he glanced down and saw blood pooling through Luke's hastily improvised bandage.

"Want me to take a look at that?" he offered. Gratefully, Luke eased off his shirt, watching as Sullivan pulled a small first aid kit from his pack and set about cleaning and covering the wound, taping the edges together and covering the whole lot with a sterile bandage.

"That will do until we get back," he assured Luke. "But I think it's going to need re-stitching."

Luke shrugged, putting his shirt back on. He'd come to that conclusion himself.

Arianna.

For the first time in a day, Luke allowed himself to think of her. He wondered how she was, thought how relieved she would be when Lucia arrived home safely, although there was no guarantee Santorini wouldn't try again.

Luke realised that from now on their lives would be lived under that permanent cloud of worry. That was assuming, of course, that Arianna allowed him back into her life.

During the past fortnight, their differences had been put aside in the face of mutual concern over Lucia. Luke wondered if now that Lucia had been safely found, Arianna could overcome her prejudices against him, or if they would still prove an insurmountable barrier.

Luke swallowed at the thought of never seeing her again. Behind him, Lucia murmured in her sleep, and Luke realised that being banished from her life would hurt almost as much as being banished from Arianna's. He marvelled at how they could have become so important to him in such a short space of time.

Arianna was sleeping. Sheer exhaustion had finally dragged her under, but it was an uneasy sleep and she cried aloud at the nightmarish images crowding her unconscious mind.

Visions of Lucia wounded, dying, or dead. Of Luke lying on the ground, shot and bleeding, her ex-husband standing over him brandishing a gun, cruel face alight with the pleasure of the kill, and overlying it all, the image of the abandoned broken swing, slowly creaking backwards and forwards…

"Mummy!" Lucia cried out to her.

In her dream, Arianna was clawing her way up a mountainside to reach her, howling in frustration as she kept slipping back painful inches, her heart pounding fit to burst with the effort of climbing.

"Mummy!" Her child was shaking her.

A part of Arianna realised it wasn't a dream and struggled up from under the blanket of unconsciousness, frantically trying to wake up.

She opened her eyes, and Lucia was there… miraculously, amazingly … she was there, scrambling onto the bed, hurling herself into her sleep-drugged mother's arms who clutched with stunned disbelief at her child, their tears mingling as Arianna finally awoke and realised it wasn't a dream. It was real. Lucia was there.

She looked over her daughter's dark head into the tear-drenched eyes of Isabella, standing in the bedroom doorway.

"Lucia!" she gasped. "You're home! Oh, thank heavens! You're home."

"It was Luke," cried Lucia, wriggling round in her mother's lap and pointing.

Arianna realised he was there, standing behind Isabella, eyes wary, shadowed with exhaustion, face dark with a day's growth of stubble, clothes grimy and bloodstained.

They stared at each other.

Tears slid down her face at the question in his eyes, understanding he was asking her to forget about what had happened, to accept him, riches, and all, and let him back into their lives.

For a moment she hesitated, longing to draw him into their family group, to take his tired head and lay it on her shoulder.

Lucia stirred in her arms, and as Arianna looked down at her small daughter something hardened inside, and all the old fears resurfaced.

She had trusted a rich man before and look at what had happened. How could she risk such a thing happening again?

Luke watched, heart in his mouth, hopeful she was going to hold out a hand to him. Her face clouded, the old suspicions crowded into her expression, and he knew he had lost her again.

"Thank you," Arianna murmured. "For bringing her home. We'll never forget what you did, never."

She saw his eyes go dark with understanding, weary acceptance on his face before he turned on his heel and left without saying a word...

~Chapter Eighteen~
"It was in his nature to be evil,"

Isabella paced like an angry jungle cat. "He risked his life for Lucia!" Arianna looked up into the darkly furious eyes of her sister-in-law, flinching away from the condemnation there.

"I know."

It was later, much later ... Lucia had been bathed, fed, petted, fussed over, hugged, and put to bed with Teddy, relieved beyond words to be back in her pretty, pink bedroom, leaving her mother to face Isabella's wrath.

"I know he risked his life, Bella, and I'm grateful, I am, very, very grateful to him, but..."

"But what?" demanded Isabella, angrily. "There is no but, Anna. You turned him away as if he were nothing, meant nothing to you."

"What did you expect?" demanded Arianna, her temper rising as the stresses and strains of the past two weeks finally took their toll.

"Did you expect me to fall on his neck and promise to spend the rest of my life with him because he saved Lucia's life?"

"Not because he saved Lucia's life, no, but because you love him," stated Isabella flatly, watching as the anger died from Arianna's face to be replaced with abject misery.

"I thought I loved him, yes," she murmured. "But he lied to me."

"Well, of course, he did, so what?" exclaimed Isabella impatiently. "You didn't give him many other options, what with this ridiculous prejudice you have against wealthy men."

"It's not ridiculous," exclaimed Arianna. "Look what happened to your brother. He was the kindest, most considerate man alive until he became wealthy, and then he changed. He became cruel and spiteful, a bully who thought nothing of hitting his wife. I can't risk going through that again or exposing Lucia to it, I simply can't."

"What?" Isabella stared at her in obvious disbelief. "Is that what you believe, Anna? That it was the money that changed Roberto?"

"Of course," replied Arianna, surprised.

"Oh, Anna." Bella slumped into a chair in dismay. "I knew you had misconceptions about Roberto, but I never realised … oh, this is all my fault. If I'd known, understood…"

"Bella?" Arianna sat opposite her sister-in-law and clasped her hand. "What is it? What's the matter? What do you mean, it's all your fault?"

Isabella drew herself up, took a deep shaky breath, and then eyed Arianna steadily.

"There's something I have to tell you, something I should have told you years ago, but the time never seemed right, and we were okay, so I didn't want to upset you unnecessarily."

She paused, bit her lip, then seemed to reach a resolution and continued.

"Our fathers, as you know, had been good friends for years. It was hoped that Roberto and you would make a good match, and I believe that's why your parents came to Italy. Your mother wanted to meet him. I envied you for having a mother who wouldn't allow her daughter to be pushed into anything against her will. My mother was so controlled by my father, I knew when he told her he'd picked out a husband for me, she'd agree. Oh, I know she loved me, both my parents loved me in their way, but my father was a strict, old-fashioned man and my life had been a very narrow and confined one."

Isabella grinned wryly at Arianna.

"What they didn't know was I'd already met someone. I was sneaking out to meet him at every opportunity I could. I knew I was risking my father's anger, but I was seventeen and thought I was invincible."

Arianna smiled at the wistful look in Isabella's eyes. "What was his name?" she asked, gently.

"Nick," replied Isabella. "He was American, nineteen years old, and travelling around Europe on a gap year. He was a waiter in a local restaurant when we met and fell in love. He asked me to go away with him, but when he realised how impossible that was, he decided to stay with me for as long as he could."

"He loved you," said Arianna, and Isabella glanced up, her heart in her eyes.

"We loved each other," she confirmed. "He was my first ... well, my first everything. My first kiss, my first boyfriend, my first ..." she paused, looking at Arianna. "My first lover," she finished.

"What happened?" she asked.

"Your parents' visit went well. They were charmed by Roberto and why not? He could put on a good act. Not even my parents knew what was beneath the handsome face and perfect manners. But I knew ... with me, his guard would drop, and then I'd see what he was like."

"I don't understand," whispered Arianna, unsettled by what she saw in Isabella's eyes.

"My brother was evil," stated Isabella flatly. "An evil, manipulative, spiteful bully. Whilst my father was alive, he had to hide it from the world, but I knew. All my life he never missed an opportunity to hurt me or make me look stupid in my parents' eyes. Oh, Isabella, why are you so clumsy, why can't you be more like your brother? Oh, Isabella, why can't you get good grades at school like your brother?"

She broke off, angrily wiping a shaking hand over her eyes.

"Then your parents came to visit. I spent many hours with them, saw the look in their eyes when they spoke of you, saw the love they had for you and was torn. I wanted Roberto to marry you, wanted you for a sister. Even though we hadn't met I already liked you, yet at the same time was afraid for you, afraid of what my brother would do to you."

She looked at Arianna.

"I'm sorry," she said. "For being too afraid to speak to them, but I'm not sure they would have believed me anyway."

Arianna nodded, her eyes never leaving Isabella's face.

"Then," she continued, "towards the end of their visit, my parents offered to fly them to Rome for the day. My father was a competent pilot, but something went wrong – the electrics on the plane, no one knows for sure. At the time I believed the official line of technical error, but now, looking back, I'm not so sure..."

"No, Bella!" gasped Arianna. "You can't believe Roberto was somehow responsible for the deaths of our parents?"

Isabella gazed steadily at her.

Arianna closed her eyes in horror, remembering all too vividly that terrible morning. She had been summoned to the headmistress's office, had seen the look of compassion in the woman's eyes and known, even before she spoke, that something dreadful had happened.

She remembered the nightmare of the double funeral, the long days when she feared she was losing her mind. Then, like a knight in shining armour, Roberto Santorini had appeared and carried her back to Italy to stay with him and his sister. It would have been their fathers' wish, he insisted, that he take care of her.

"Do you remember when we first met, Anna? When Roberto brought you to Italy to stay with us after the funerals, and you met his sister ... his sister with the broken arm?"

"You'd broken it falling off the back of your friend's motorbike," replied Arianna with a smile.

"No, I didn't," said Isabella, slowly.

"But I don't understand. That's what both you and Roberto told me, why would you..."

Arianna broke off as Isabella continued to look steadily at her, saw the truth in her eyes, cold realisation drenching her soul.

"Bella? Oh no, Bella! You don't mean ... Roberto broke your arm?"

Isabella nodded, and Arianna's hand flew to her mouth in horror.

"But why? Why would he do such a terrible thing?"

"With our parents dead he no longer had to hide his true nature. He controlled my every move, and it became difficult for me to see Nick. I think Roberto suspected there was someone, but he couldn't prove it. Then Nick asked me to leave with him. I'd told him you see, told him everything, he knew how afraid I was."

A lone tear slipped down Isabella's face. Angrily, she wiped it away and continued with her story.

"He worried each time I had to go back to that house, was scared for me. He made plans for us to disappear. It only had to be for six months until I was eighteen and inherited my share of my father's estate, then I would be independent and could do what I liked."

Isabella took a deep breath.

"It was agreed that Nick would come for me at midnight on his motorbike, that part at least was true. Somehow, Roberto knew. He must have been having me watched. When I left my room to go to Nick and escape that dreadful place, he was waiting for me. He told me I would never see Nick again, and that he had arranged for me to be sent to a finishing school far away in the mountains. Somehow, I found the courage to stand up to him, told him I was leaving and there was nothing he could do about it. I tried to go, but he gripped my left arm, looked me straight in the eye and smiled, I'll never forget that smile to my dying day or the madness in his eyes as he twisted my arm back and snapped it…"

Arianna gasped in horror and tightened her grip on Isabella's hand.

"When I was on my knees sobbing with pain, he dragged me to a table where there was paper and a pen ready and he made me write a note to Nick, a horrible, cruel note, telling him it was over, that I never wanted to see him again. I pleaded with him, refused to do it, but he threatened to kill me, and so help me god I believed him. I wrote the note. He went to Nick who was waiting at the gates, gave him the note and told him heaven only knows what. As I lay on the floor crying, I heard the motorbike roar away into the night and I never saw him again."

"Oh, Bella," whispered Arianna, tears welling.

"Then, a few days later," continued Isabella, "he brought you back and told me he intended to marry you. If I knew what was good for me, I'd better keep my mouth shut about anything that might upset you, and I did, I was too afraid to do anything else and for that, I'm so sorry."

"It's all right, Bella. I understand."

"I watched as he acted the concerned, loving suitor," Isabella continued. "In your grief and innocence, you fell for it, unknowing and unsuspecting. You married, we re-located to England, I inherited my money and at last, was free. But by then it was too late, too late for me or you. I could have run, I suppose, escaped to anywhere in the world, maybe even have found Nick. But I couldn't. In the brief time, I'd known you I'd grown to love you and was afraid to leave you completely at his mercy."

Isabella gazed steadily at Arianna.

"So, I stayed, and as his façade began to slip, his true nature emerged. Lucia was born, another reason to stay, and then one day I saw a look in your eyes and knew he'd hit you for the first time. Still, you stayed, your loyalty and refusal to admit defeat keeping you with him. Then he embezzled all that money, and I was afraid you might go with him out of some misguided sense of wifely duty."

"But how could I have done?" asked Arianna, confused. "He never told me what he was planning, I didn't know, none of us knew …" Her voice trailed off at the look in Isabella's eyes.

"Bella," she breathed. "Did you know?"

"No," Isabella hastily reassured her. "I had a feeling he was planning something but not that, never that. No. Do you remember that day, the day he left? You phoned and asked if I could mind Lucia for an hour or so whilst you went to the hairdressers."

"I remember," murmured Arianna. "You took her to the park, but it was raining so you brought her home early."

"That's right," agreed Isabella. "We got back before you, and that's when I found his note."

"Roberto left me a note?" Arianna stared at Isabella in confusion. "What did it say?"

"He ordered you to bring Lucia and your passport and meet him. He was going to take you with him on the run to South America." She looked Arianna directly in the eye.

"I couldn't let that happen, Anna. I didn't know what he'd done but knew if he took you out of the country you'd be completely at his mercy, and I wouldn't be able to protect you. I destroyed his note. When you got back, I lied, told you Roberto had called to say he wouldn't be home that night, took you both back to my house to stay the night, and the next day..."

"The next day, the police came," finished Arianna. "And the nightmare began."

"Should I have given you that note, Anna?" Isabella asked.

Arianna frowned as she considered, then slowly shook her head.

"I don't know," she murmured. "I don't know what I would have done. I don't think I would have gone with him, but... I'm grateful to you I never had to make that choice."

"So," concluded Isabella. "Do you see how unfair you've been to Luke? You believed it was money that changed Roberto, but he was rotten from birth. The money had nothing to do with the way he behaved. It was in his nature to be evil, the same as it's in Luke's nature to be kind."

"I ... I don't know," Arianna stuttered, confused. "I don't know what to think."

"I think you've sent away a good and honest man," stated Isabella, firmly. "One who loves you and Lucia, and one who risked his life to save your child."

Arianna stared at her sister-in-law in silence, a silence that stretched between them and was only shattered when the phone began to ring.

Isabella waited, but Arianna continued to sit. Impatiently, Isabella answered the phone.

"Yes? No, it's Isabella. What? What did you say?" she paused, a surprised and immensely satisfied expression crossing her face.

"Yes," she agreed. "That is amazing news, yes, I'll tell her, okay, goodbye."

She hung up and raised her brows at Arianna.

"That was Luke," she said, and Arianna's eyes widened in enquiry.

"He wanted to let us know he's had a phone call from his contact at New Scotland Yard. Roberto was found dumped in their car park this morning, bound and drugged, with a note pinned to his clothes saying here is Roberto Santorini, a gift from an anonymous friend."

"What?" Arianna gasped in shock. "But … but how? Who put him there?"

"I have absolutely no idea," replied Isabella, her dark eyes glittering with satisfaction.

"No idea at all…"

~Chapter Nineteen~
"Where is he?"

Sleep eluded Arianna that night, as the shocking events of the day kept her wide-eyed and staring at the ceiling, tossing, and turning on her pillow. Conflicting emotions and thoughts warring and clashing in her tired and confused mind.

Isabella's tale had affected her deeply. She imagined what Isabella had been through, the look on her face when she spoke of Nick, the love lost to her forever. Realising Isabella would forever be scarred by his loss, Arianna's anger boiled at her ex-husband.

"Bastard," she muttered, and that brought her thoughts around to Isabella's statement that it hadn't been money that changed Roberto. He was born evil, and it was someone's nature that determined their behaviour, not wealth or the lack of it.

At dawn, Arianna gave up and rose from her rumpled bed, stumbling blearily into the shower in the hope it would shake the clouds of confusion from her brain. Lucia was still sleeping soundly, and Arianna decided to let her lie in, imagining how exhausted her daughter must be after her ordeal.

She brewed coffee and curled up to drink it, turning the situation over in her head, thinking … wondering what Luke was doing, her heart aching at the thought of him.

Just after eight, the doorbell sounded. Arianna jerked upright, spilling coffee onto her jeans with a mumbled curse, and rushed to the door, heart pounding, convinced it was Luke.

Eagerly, she pulled open the door. A woman stood there. A stranger, yet she looked familiar, her piercing blue gaze so like Luke's that even before she spoke Arianna knew who she was.

"Hello, Arianna," she said. "I'm Susannah Blackwood, Luke's sister. Can I talk to you?"

Wordlessly, Arianna stepped back to allow Luke's sister access, flinching as Susannah's eyes travelled around the small interior.

"Luke said your home was charming," she said and smiled at Arianna – a shy, nervous smile that made Arianna like her very much.

"Would you like some coffee?" she murmured, and Susannah's eyes brightened.

"Please," she said.

Grateful for something to do, Arianna hurried to the kitchen to pour her a cup, as Susannah settled herself gracefully into a chair. She looked so like Luke; a younger, softer, feminine version of him. It made Arianna's heart catch in her chest looking at her, and as she poured the coffee her hand shook, spilling it onto the worktop.

She sat in the chair opposite Susannah and watched the other woman appreciatively sip her coffee, noting the sadness in her eyes. She remembered Luke mentioning that his sister's marriage had fallen apart the year before.

Resolutely, Susannah put her cup down and gazed steadily at Arianna.

"This is hard," she murmured. "I shouldn't be here but have so much to say to you, I don't know where to start. I guess, maybe, it all boils down to the fact you've hurt my brother unnecessarily, at least as far as I can see, and I suppose I wanted to ask you why."

"I'm sorry," stuttered Arianna, rather taken aback at the other woman's directness. "I never meant to hurt him, it was the last thing I ever intended, but ..." She took a deep breath.

"When I found out he'd lied to me about the money it triggered bad memories for me. It seemed better, safer even, to not see him again. I was angry he'd lied to me, felt so foolish ..." Her voice trailed away. Helplessly she looked into the kindly sympathetic eyes of Luke's sister.

"I understand," she said. "And believe me, I've told him how wrong he was, that he should have told you the truth from the beginning. I've seen women come and go in my brother's life, Arianna, some he liked a lot..."

Susannah paused and grinned. "There were even some I liked a lot, yet when the relationship was over, he remained untouched, ready to move on. But this time, well, I sat up most of last night talking with Luke and I've never seen such a look of complete and utter despair in his eyes. A look you put there, Arianna." Susannah gazed levelly at her, and Arianna edged away from the other woman's honesty.

"I can't bear to know he's suffering and not try to make things right for him, because he's my big brother and I love him. He's always looked out for me; I guess it's time I returned the favour."

"Luke is very lucky," murmured Arianna, feeling tears prick at her eyelids, "to have a sister like you. I wish …" She broke off and studied her hands, hearing a slight rustle as Susannah leant forward and gently placed a warm hand over her cold, shaking ones.

"It's okay to be scared, Arianna," she said. "You've been alone for such a very long time, and I know how good a mother you've been to Lucia. But I also know how much my brother loves you both and he would never hurt you, not in a million years." She paused.

"Did Luke ever tell you how he came to start ICRA?" Confused by the abrupt conversational shift, Arianna shook her head.

"My mother has a friend, her best friend, they've known each other since they were children. For a long time, my mother believed her friend would never marry, but she did. A man she met through work, an Iranian who was living in England. I know my mother had concerns, but her friend seemed so happy, and as the years passed and they had two gorgeous children, we all relaxed." Susannah's eyes grew hard.

"Then the marriage started to go wrong, and one day she came home from work to find them gone. He'd taken the children back to his family in Iran."

Arianna slowly nodded. "I've heard of such things happening," she agreed.

"He refused to send the children back, let her know where they were, or even let her speak to them. He told her they were lost to her forever and that she would no longer be considered their mother. She was devastated, and of course, we went to the police, but they said there was little they could do to help."

Susannah sighed, lost in her story. "In the end, Luke couldn't bear it anymore, so he took matters into his own hands. Without telling anyone his intentions, he began to look for the children himself. It took him months to track them down. He didn't have the experience or the contacts he has now, and it took him months to plan their recovery, but he finally did it. He brought those children home to their mother. I think in that moment of reunion, he found his true vocation."

Susannah's eyes smiled gently at the memory.

"So, you see, Arianna," she continued, "you have nothing to fear. You can trust Luke. Because although he is more than capable of looking out for himself, and others, and let's face it, would you want a man who couldn't, he would never hurt you. It's not in his nature."

"I think, maybe, that's something I'm beginning to realise," replied Arianna. "I lost both my parents when I was only eighteen and was married within a few weeks of their funeral. I never had a chance to experience life. Looking back, I understand now how naïve and emotionally unprepared I was." She paused, and Susannah squeezed her hands encouragingly.

"I took everything Roberto, my husband, said at face value, never thought to question him, never dreamt he might not be exactly the way he portrayed himself. A few months after we were married, he inherited his parents' money and accepted a job working for Bank Italia in their London branch. I was thrilled for him. He'd worked so hard to get the position, and I was pleased to be coming back to England." Arianna paused, remembering.

"Italy was beautiful, fascinating, and of course wherever Roberto lived was home to me. But England is in my heart, it's where I feel familiar. We moved back to London, bought an amazing house and started living the good life, at least as far as material things went."

Arianna looked at Susannah who was silently listening, eyes intently focused on her face, encouraging her to continue.

"That's when it all started to go wrong. Slowly, at first, he began to change. Everything I did or said annoyed him. I tried so hard to please him, but it was never good enough. I was never good enough ... He constantly picked at me, finding fault, correcting me, until I began to doubt everything I did or said, and my self-confidence was completely eroded."

"What happened then?" Susannah urged when Arianna fell silent.

"I fell pregnant with Lucia," she sighed. "For a little while things seemed to improve, but it was only temporary. After she was born, he became worse, until finally the inevitable happened and he became violent towards me."

"That must have been very difficult for you," commented Susannah softly, when Arianna stopped and gulped at her coffee.

"It was," agreed Arianna. "On the one hand I couldn't bring myself to admit to anyone my marriage was a failure, and I was so afraid. I had no other family, you see, apart from Roberto and his sister, Isabella. No one to turn to, no one to help me or even go to for advice. But on the other hand, I wasn't so innocent I didn't know the first punch is the hardest. After that, it only gets easier." She swallowed, unable to look at the sympathy she saw in Susannah's eyes.

"I worried about it for weeks, then came home one day and he'd gone. The police came, and I guess Luke has told you the rest."

"Yes, he did," Susannah nodded. "He told me last night. Some of it when we were sitting in A&E waiting to be seen, and the rest after I'd taken him home."

"A&E?" Arianna's head snapped up. "What were you doing in A&E? Is Luke all right? Is he hurt? Did Roberto hurt him?"

She sprang up in her chair, her eyes wide and panicking, and Susannah quickly put a comforting hand on her arm.

"Arianna, relax," she ordered, although a small, satisfied smile played around her mouth at Arianna's obvious distress.

"He's fine. His little adventure re-opened his wound and I insisted he had it seen to. It needed re-stitching, but he's fine."

"Good, that's good," gasped Arianna, sinking back down into her chair and burying her head in her hands.

"Oh," she moaned between her fingers. "I don't know what to do."

"Well, I know what you should do," said a small voice behind them.

Both women sharply turned to see Lucia, sleepy in her pink nightshirt, standing in the doorway to her basement bedroom, her eyes fixed on her mother.

"Lucia, sweetheart, how long have you been standing there?" Arianna began.

"Long enough," her daughter replied, her eyes showing wisdom beyond her years. "Long enough to know what you should do. You should go to Luke…"

"Lucia…" Arianna interrupted helplessly.

"Go to him," insisted her daughter. "Tell him how sorry you are, get down on one knee and ask him to marry us."

"Oh Lucia," sighed Arianna. "It's not that simple…"

"Why isn't it?" asked Susannah and smiled as Arianna gaped at her. "Do you love my brother?" she demanded when Arianna remained speechless.

"I, well … I …" gasped Arianna.

"Do you love my brother?" Susannah asked urgently. Arianna hesitated, her cheeks flushing, aware of Lucia's hopeful gaze.

"Yes," she finally gave in and admitted. "Yes, I love him."

She looked at Susannah, and Luke's sister felt hope leap into her heart at the resolve in the other woman's eyes.

"I love him," she repeated, and a look of wonder crept onto her face. "Where is he?" she demanded.

A smile crossed Susannah's face. "I'll take you to him," she said, simply.

~Chapter Twenty~
"Did you just growl at me?"

Was it acceptable for a man to have a beer at ten in the morning? Luke stared morosely into his fridge in search of breakfast. Empty shelves leered back, and the champagne bought in readiness to drink after dinner on Arianna's birthday mocked his aloneness.

Damn it, he decided and reached for a can. A man could drink what the hell he pleased, when the hell he pleased, especially considering the day and night he'd had.

Luke winced as his side throbbed, reluctantly remembered the medication he was on and the strict instructions of the doctor, threw the can back in the fridge and slammed the door shut.

For a moment, he allowed himself to think of Arianna. He pulled his mobile from his jeans pocket and examined the call log, but apart from messages from Marcus and Susannah logged the previous evening, the phone had remained stubbornly silent all night.

Who the hell are you kidding? She's not going to call. Accept that and move on. Angrily, he switched the phone off, tossed it onto the kitchen table, and limped back into the lounge easing himself onto the sofa, waves of exhaustion threatening to drag him under.

He sighed and laid his head back. Perhaps he should give in and hit the sack, catch up with his sleep, and then, and then … and then he'd think of something else to do.

Luke closed his eyes, the silence of the apartment pressing onto his eardrums as he shifted, desperately trying to find a position that didn't make him feel as though his side was being stepped on by a large, heavy animal.

And into the quietness came a tiny sound – a shy, hesitant knock at the door.

Luke opened his eyes, frowning. His apartment came fully equipped with lobby service. Visitors had to gain clearance before being admitted unless they had a key to the lift, and only his family had keys.

He groaned, praying it wasn't his mother, unable to face the thought of a dose of maternal cosseting just then. He crawled off the sofa and went to the door. Peering through the spyhole, he nearly collapsed with shock.

It was Arianna.

He opened the door and caught the look of uncertainty in her eyes when she saw him. Not knowing, why she was there, or what the best thing was to say, Luke opted for saying nothing and simply stepped back to allow her access.

Slowly, hesitantly, she entered. He heard her follow him as he stalked down the hall and into the lounge. Turning to face her, he saw her eyes widen as she looked around the spacious, open-plan living space, and the solid wall of glass doors opening onto a balcony twice the size of her tiny home, with its stunning, eye-grabbing view across the skyline of London.

"This is amazing," she murmured and flashed him a shy smile. "How small my house must have seemed, compared to ..." she gestured with her hand, "all this ..." she finished, and her hand dropped back to her side.

"It's not the space people live in, but the people living in the space that makes a home," he informed her curtly, watching as she was irresistibly drawn over to the view.

"Still," she commented pragmatically. "It can't hurt to come home to it." She shot him another hesitant smile. He continued to stare stonily at her. The smile slipped, and insecurity flickered in her eyes.

"Why are you here, Arianna?" he asked bluntly, and she winced from his directness.

"I was concerned about you," she murmured. "I wanted to check you were okay, and I didn't get a chance to thank you, not properly, for all you've done for Lucia and me..."

"Consider me thanked," he snapped, eyes flashing with annoyance. "And as you can see, I'm fine, so if that was all you came for?"

"No, Luke ... I..." Arianna hesitated, understanding the barrier he had placed between them. "I'm sorry," she finally whispered into the silence. "I'm so sorry, Luke."

"What, exactly, are you apologising for, Arianna?" Luke asked, cautiously.

"For misjudging you," she replied, lifting her chin, facing him squarely in the eyes, sudden determination flooding through her. She would get this out, she would say this, and then, well ... then it would be down to him.

"I allowed my bad experience with Roberto to prejudice me against all men, but particularly rich ones. I was too young and naïve to fully understand that sudden wealth will only bring out the character already there. Roberto was always evil, I know that now, but for years believed it was the money that changed him. In a way, I had to convince myself it was the truth."

"Why?" demanded Luke. The question was curt, yet his tone was gentler, less abrasive.

"Because to admit to anything else would mean I'd made a huge mistake, that I'd allowed myself to be fooled by charming manners and a handsome face."

"He's not that handsome," muttered Luke.

Arianna smiled, relieved at his touch of humour. "No," she agreed. "He's not... not compared to you, anyway." She hesitated, fascinated, and touched by the faint, self-conscious flush that coloured his face.

"It was unfair of me to compare you to Roberto, and I wanted to say I was sorry. That's why I'm here." Arianna stumbled to a halt, tripping over her tongue, and wishing Luke would say something, anything, rather than continue to stand there, staring at her, eyes hooded and unyielding of what, if anything, he was thinking or feeling.

"I see," he finally said, and Arianna raised hopeful eyes. "That's why you're here? To apologise to me. Well, apology accepted Arianna, now you can go."

"But I ..." began Arianna, shocked speechless as Luke took her by the arm, led her down the hall to the door, opened it and pushed her through into the plush corridor outside.

"Thank you very much for the apology, goodbye," he declared grimly, and Arianna found herself staring once more at the shut door, the echo of its slam still reverberating in her ears.

Mutely, she walked to the bank of elevators, pressing the button on the nearest one. He had rejected her, thrown her bodily out of his apartment. He'd not given her a chance to explain herself, he'd just ... Arianna's eyes narrowed. A growl rumbled deep in her throat.

No, she was not going to let him get away with this. How dare he toss her out as if she were no more than a sack of dirty laundry! The elevator light stopped at her floor and the doors pinged as they slid gracefully open.

Why that, smug, arrogant, supercilious...

"Bastard!"

Arianna spat the expletive out between gritted teeth, and the elderly, well-dressed couple exiting the elevator shot her an alarmed glance. Arianna stormed back along the corridor and thundered on his door with her fists.

"Blackwood!" she howled. "Open the door this minute!" For good measure, she also gave the door a hefty kick.

Luke opened the door, his face a mask of surprise. Arianna shoved rudely past him, slamming the door behind her, whirling to face him, eyes snapping fire in a face alive with irritated animation.

"Don't you ever ... *ever*," she snarled, "throw me out of your apartment again!"

"I thought you'd finished," he drawled, leaning against the wall, arms crossed, the thought flying through his brain he had never seen her look so beautiful.

"Well, I hadn't!" she snapped.

Luke shrugged, hope hammering at his heart as Arianna paced angrily up and down the hall, eyes narrowing further every time she glanced in his direction.

"I had something to say to you," she spat. "Something important!"

"So, say it."

"I will…"

"Okay." Luke waited patiently, listening as Arianna's quick, angry breaths echoed in the silence, wondering if she'd be able to say it and determined not to say it first.

"I'm waiting …" he drawled mildly, then blinked with surprise. "Did you just growl at me?" he enquired.

"So, what if I did?" snapped Arianna. "A woman is entitled to growl when faced by a man as obnoxious, obtuse, and downright annoying as you!"

"Darling, I'm flattered," he deadpanned, beginning to enjoy himself.

"Don't be," she cautioned. "They weren't compliments. I don't think I've ever met such a pig-headed, insensitive lump of a man. I don't know why I…"

"Why you what?" asked Luke, drawing himself upright in sudden, agonising anticipation.

"Why I … I…"

"Yes?" he insisted, urgently. "Why you what?"

"Why I love you!" she all but screamed at him, and Luke closed his eyes in relief.

"Well, it's about bloody time," he growled back, and Arianna found herself pressed against the wall as strong arms trapped her, and his hungry mouth fastened greedily onto hers.

For a split second her body fought him, struggling against his superior strength, until her befuddled brain managed to get the message through that this was precisely where she wanted to be, and her arms crept up around his neck, her body melding into his.

A soft moan escaped her lips as his mouth left hers and his teeth nipped gently at her jaw, sending shockwaves of dazed pleasure racing through every cell in her body, igniting and exploding until the flames were raging all around, consuming and overwhelming every conscious thought and she was nothing more than a bundle of aching nerve endings, existing purely in a universe of ultimate sensation.

Need, want ... urgent and raw, it had her hands ripping at his shirt, eyes darkening with desire, her breath heaving in short, harsh gasps.

Luke groaned as her small white teeth fastened onto his neck. He pulled back, saw the inner fire raging in her eyes and his self-control snapped.

He lifted her, dimly she felt her sandals drop from her feet, her hands fisting in his hair, dragging his face back to hers as she wrapped her legs around his waist, thrilling to the feel of his strong arms holding her securely, carrying her down the hallway.

He kicked open the shut door to his bedroom, and Arianna had a confused impression of a spacious and light room, masculine in muted cream and chocolate tones, then they were at the bed, falling onto its vast, welcoming expanse.

"I love you," Arianna gasped. "Oh Luke, I love you so much."

Luke groaned in response. Pulling away, he cupped her face in his powerfully tender hands, stroking her hair back. Studied her face so intently that she blushed under his scrutiny.

"I knew it was you," he murmured. "Right from that very first moment we met. It was your eyes. I knew then it would always be you. Arianna Santorini, I love every inch of you, and I always will. It's like I've come home. You're my home. You, and Lucia."

Hot tears spurted at his words, and a sob erupted from her chest. Dismayed, he held her close. "Don't cry, please don't, what have I done? I never meant to make you cry."

She smiled at him through the tears. "They're tears of happiness," she reassured him. "I never thought, never imagined..." Pulling herself together, she gathered him to her, forehead to forehead, eyes so close they could only see the glitter of each other's souls.

"I love you," she whispered. "I never thought I would ever, could ever, feel this way about someone, the way I feel about you..." unable to find the words, she nipped gently at his mouth. "I love you..."

The look in Luke's eyes when he finally pulled away long moments later, was enough to make her want to cry again. Tenderly, he lay a hand on the buttons of her dress.

"Is this, all right?" he asked, hesitantly, shyly.

"Oh yes," she reassured him. "It's all right. But what about your wound?"

"Be gentle with me, then," he whispered. "And it'll be fine."

And it was...

~Chapter Twenty-One~
"Don't you hurt him!"

Midday sunlight was casting slanting shadows over the bedroom floor when Arianna drifted back to the surface to find him still by her side, a strong arm gently cocooning her. A quilt had been pulled over them and she blinked sleepily at him, mortified she had fallen asleep, concerned he would be insulted or hurt by her action.

"I'm sorry," she murmured.

He looked down and smiled. "Hello, sleeping beauty."

Arianna rubbed at heavy eyes. "How long?" she asked.

Luke chuckled at the worry in her voice. "Not long," he reassured her. "About an hour."

"Hmm," sighed Arianna, pulling herself into a sitting position, flexing out the cramp in a foot kept too long in an awkward position.

"I'm sorry," she said again.

Luke's smile slipped at the panic in her voice.

"Arianna," he began. "It's okay, I'm not cross with you for falling asleep. If you want the truth, I drifted off myself. It's been a long, few weeks for all of us; it's only natural you're exhausted."

Arianna studied him for a moment, then allowed herself to relax and smile at the complete lack of blame or annoyance in his eyes.

"I love you," she murmured.

His eyes darkened with desire, and he pulled her close, holding her tightly against his chest.

"I love you too," he declared, then pulled back and studied her with a frown.

"But what made you change your mind, I mean when I brought Lucia back you more or less ordered me out of your life, I thought I'd never hear from you again."

"Oh, a pair of sisters managed to knock some sense into me," she muttered, and at his confused look she shook her head. "It doesn't matter," she insisted, and laughed happily, trailing her hand lightly down his arm.

"Speaking of Lucia, where is she? Is she somewhere safe?" Luke asked, and Arianna was warmed by the concern in his voice.

"She's with Isabella, she's fine," she reassured him and felt him relax beneath her.

"If she's with Isabella then I'm sure she'll be safe, no matter what," he muttered dryly.

Arianna looked at him, puzzled by his cryptic comment. "What do you mean by that?" she asked.

Luke hesitated, then shook his head. "It doesn't matter," he assured her, unsure whether it would be prudent to share his suspicions about her sister-in-law, not even sure whether the wild conclusions he had come to about Isabella Santorini could be correct.

"Where are you going?" he asked, as Arianna slithered from the bed and picked her dress up from the floor.

"I need to stretch my legs," she explained. "I think I slept wrong, my foot is all crampy, plus I want to have another look at your amazing balcony. I don't think I've ever been so high above the city and that view looked incredible."

Lazily, Luke struggled out of bed and pulled on his jeans, leaving them unbuttoned so they rode low over his taut hips. Arianna felt a hot jolt of desire course thickly through her veins.

One quick look at the view, she promised herself, then this man was going to be dragged back to bed again, kicking, and screaming all the way if needs be.

Hand in hand they wandered through the vast lounge and out the still open doors onto the large terrace.

Stunned by its sophisticated beauty, Arianna let her hand trail over the lush green vegetation, admiring the dark teak furniture, and raising her brows at the industrial-looking barbecue that would have dominated her tiny garden, yet here nestled snugly along the low wall surrounding the balcony.

She leant on the wall, bricks warm beneath her palms, gazing across the magnificent cityscape. Shading her eyes against the sun, she looked westward to see Big Ben and the Houses of Parliament in the distance, and the Millennium Eye looking like a child's toy glinting in the midday sun.

"What an amazing view," she gasped. Luke dropped an arm around her waist, pulling her close to his bare chest, his chin resting on the top of her head.

"It is pretty good," he admitted, nuzzling into her neck, and kissing the soft, tender spot behind her ear.

"Fancy some champagne?" he asked.

Arianna blinked in surprise. "Do you have any?" she asked.

"I believe there's a bottle lurking somewhere in the fridge," he grinned mischievously.

Arianna smiled, reaching up to press a warm, loving kiss to his cheek.

"I think that would be great," she whispered in his ear. "Maybe we could take it back to bed with us?"

"Arianna Santorini," he gasped, feigning outraged shock. "Twice in one day?"

"Get used to it," she ordered, nipping at his jaw with her teeth, satisfied by the look of absolute lust which darkened his eyes and tightened his mouth.

A phone rang in the apartment, and they pulled apart, grinning ruefully at one another.

"Your mobile?" Arianna asked.

Luke shook his head. "No, it's my landline," he looked around and frowned. "Not sure where my mobile is, I think I left it in the kitchen."

"Well," began Arianna, running her hand over his chest. "Why don't you answer the phone, I'll open the champagne, and then I'll meet you in the bedroom."

"I could let the machine get it," he offered, and she smiled and kissed him again before pulling away and stepping back towards the doors.

"It might be important," she said over her shoulder. "And besides, it'll give me a chance to snoop around."

He followed her in and reached for the phone.

"Yes?" he said distractedly, and the familiar booming voice of Chief Inspector Williams, his contact at New Scotland Yard, echoed down the line.

"Blackwood, been trying your mobile for ages, we've got trouble."

"Trouble?" Luke's body snapped to attention. "What kind of trouble?"

Humming softly to herself, Arianna wandered into the large kitchen which she found on the opposite side of the hall, allowing her gaze to wander with pleasure over its gleaming grey surfaces and shining, obviously little-used appliances.

She smiled when she saw the familiar shape of Luke's mobile lying on the long, pale wood table. She picked it up intending to take it to him. Noting it was switched off, she slipped it into the deep pocket concealed in the folds of the dress she had replaced her coffee-splattered jeans with.

Opening the fridge, she tutted at its contents, wondering how a man could hope to keep body and soul together on beer, olives, and cheese. Shaking her head at the complete lack of anything nourishing or healthy in the entire vast fridge, she thought with pleasure about cooking for Luke, and finally being able to have large family meals.

In the taxi, Susannah had told her a little about their family, and Arianna had formed an impression of a slightly eccentric, yet close-knit clan, and she longed to be part of them, hoping they would all turn out to be as friendly and welcoming as Susannah.

Locating the champagne, Arianna pulled it from the rack and stepped away from the fridge. Closing the door, she turned, the smile freezing on her face, the hum choking in her throat.

"Hello, Arianna," said Roberto from his position in the doorway.

She gasped, opened her mouth to scream for Luke, and then stopped at the cold feel of the gun he pushed into her forehead.

"Oh, I wouldn't," he cautioned. "I really wouldn't." He took the gun from her head, now she stared into its black mouth, fear gripping her heart.

Slowly, Arianna set the champagne down on the table and gazed into the eyes of the husband she hadn't seen for over six years, noticing the changes in him.

He was thinner, his hair was greyer, and his eyes … it was as if he no longer had to hide the rottenness which dwelt in his heart from the outside world anymore. Now it was plain for all to see, the madness in his expression.

Arianna fought to swallow down her fear.

"Roberto," she raised her chin, staring levelly at him. "What are you doing here?"

"I've come to collect what's mine," he stated, and terror clutched her throat as he stepped closer.

"You've been a bad girl, Arianna," he purred silkily. "You've been an unfaithful wife, and I am no longer prepared to tolerate it. Do you know," he continued, as Arianna remained silent, staring mutely at him with wide, panicked eyes.

"In some countries, a husband is within his rights to kill a wife who betrays her wedding vows, and the man she has been untrue to him with."

"Don't you hurt him!" she gasped and saw cold calculation leap into his eyes.

"So," he murmured. "It's not just a fling. There are feelings involved. Good, that means you'll suffer more when you're back by my side knowing you'll never see him again."

"I'm not going anywhere with you," Arianna spat hotly, eyes blazing with outrage.

"Oh, but you will," he assured her. "If you don't, I'll simply render you unconscious, shoot your lover, and carry you to the car I have waiting. By the time you come to, we'll be far away, and you'll have to live with the knowledge that Blackwood is dead because of you."

"No," she gasped, horror hammering at her temples. "You wouldn't…"

"Oh, but I would," he promised. "Believe me, it would be a pleasure, I have a score to settle with Blackwood."

His eyes darkened, and Arianna shivered at the malice she saw there.

"Please," she whispered. "I'll do whatever you want, just please, don't hurt him."

"I'm so glad you've decided to be reasonable. But first …" he stepped forward, and Arianna cried out as his hand cracked viciously across her face, sending her flying back against the wall and crashing to the ground, pain exploding from a split lip.

Putting a hand shakily to her mouth, her fingers came away all bloody and she stared at Roberto in shock.

"You are my wife," he informed her tersely. "You even so much as look at another man again, and I will strip every inch of skin from your faithless body. Do you understand me?"

Mutely she nodded, watching as he moved to the doorway and peered cautiously into the deserted hallway.

Frantically, she stared at the blood splattering onto her hand, mind racing. Somehow, she had to let Luke know what had happened to her.

Quickly, she wiped her finger on the cool tiled floor, touching her finger back to her lip for more blood. She made her mark, then climbed shakily to her feet, praying as he turned back that he wouldn't look down, wouldn't notice.

"Come on," he ordered, roughly gripping her arm.

As he dragged her from the kitchen, Arianna fought the urge to glance down in case he followed her gaze and realised what she had done.

Stumbling, she allowed him to lead her to the door which she saw he had somehow managed to open.

She gave a final, despairing look backwards as he pulled her through, closed it behind them, and forced her along the corridor towards the elevators.

~Chapter Twenty-Two~
"You will not touch me!"

"What do you mean, he's managed to escape?" Luke spat the words out in an angry frenzy unable to believe his ears. Instinctively he stepped onto the balcony and slid shut the soundproof glass doors behind him, not wanting Arianna to hear and start panicking at the news that her murderous husband was on the loose.

"What the hell happened, Williams?"

"He was being transferred." The Chief Inspector's voice was strained and old. "The transport was ambushed, I don't know how anyone knew it was him we were moving, but my gut tells me I've got a leak somewhere in my department."

"Didn't any of the officers transferring him try to stop him from escaping?" demanded Luke.

"Of course, they did," snapped Williams, waspishly. "But the ambushers were armed. I now have the unpleasant task of visiting three sets of wives and telling them their husbands won't be coming home tonight."

Luke heard the anger in his voice. "Shit," he said.

There was silence from Williams, indicating he shared the sentiment.

"Anyway," he continued. "Santorini's probably left the country by now if he's got any sense that is, but…"

"But …" Luke continued slowly. "He might not have done."

"No," agreed Williams tersely. "He might not have done, which is why I thought I'd better call and tell you immediately. What do you think? Is he likely to go after the child again, or maybe the wife?"

"Arianna's here with me," Luke said, and there was a pregnant pause on the other end.

"I see," replied Williams briskly. "So, she's safe enough for now. What about the child?"

"She's with her aunt, Isabella Santorini," said Luke.

"Is it possible she's been in communication with her brother?" Williams asked.

Luke hesitated, remembering the boiling hatred in Isabella's eyes when she spoke of her brother, and the unsettling memory of dark eyes staring through the mask of a balaclava.

"No," he said decisively. "I think if Santorini ever contacted her, she'd tell him to go to hell, that's if she didn't kill him first. But he may go after Lucia again. We know he's been having the family watched for years so he'd know where Isabella lives."

"I better send some men around," Williams stated, and Luke nodded.

"Could you hold on just a moment," he asked, as a sudden inexplicable urge to see Arianna gripped him. "I need to check something."

He heard Williams murmur an assent as he padded barefooted across the terrace and slid open the doors. Listening, he stepped into the lounge, hearing nothing.

"Arianna?" he called, then wandered into the bedroom, the first stirring sensations of alarm dancing along his spine at the sight of the still, silent room and the empty bed rumpled from their earlier lovemaking.

They took the elevator all the way down to the car park, Arianna struggling not to show her terror as Roberto dragged her out, the concrete cold under her bare feet. A dark car screeched up beside them and a grim-faced man, menacing in his hugeness, climbed out of the back seat, flicking Arianna a carelessly contemptuous look as Roberto pushed her towards the vehicle.

"Get in," he ordered, then turned to the man. "Upstairs, penthouse suite," he commanded, curtly. "Finish the job." The man nodded brusquely and stepped into the elevator.

"What do you mean?" cried Arianna. "You don't mean ... you can't! You promised if I came quietly, you wouldn't hurt him!"

"I lied," Roberto informed her, a smirk of amused cruelty crossing his face at her horror.

"Bastard!"

She screamed and launched herself against him, clawing at his face and eyes, only subsiding, wide-eyed and sobbing with impotent rage when he held the gun against her throat, its coldness pressing against her frantically racing pulse.

"Why?" she whispered.

He gripped her arm and roughly threw her onto the back seat, quickly sliding in afterwards, the doors automatically locking as the nameless, faceless thug in the front gunned the engine and the car sped away.

"Because he touched what is rightfully mine," he spat, face twisted with venomous fury. "For that, he must die."

Arianna shrank back against the door; fear for Luke and for herself draining all the will to fight from her body.

"Arianna?" Luke called her name again, moving swiftly into the kitchen and finding it empty apart from the bottle of champagne standing on the table. The vague sensation of alarm tripled into full-blown panic. Looking wildly around the room, his eyes dropped to the floor, saw the mark, and knew for certain what had happened.

Grimly, he put the phone back to his ear. "He's been here," he snapped. "He's taken her!"

"What?" demanded Williams, concern thickening his voice. "Are you sure?"

"Oh yes," Luke knelt, fingers hovering above the capital R standing out in vivid, red blood against the cream tiled floor. "I'm sure. The bastard's got her all right."

He straightened and looked at the champagne bottle standing in isolation on the table, frowning as a memory nagged and a vision superimposed itself over his eyes.

"I'll put out an all-points," Williams was saying. "But, without knowing what type of vehicle he's in and which direction he's headed in, there's no way of tracking him."

"Oh yes there is," Luke replied, fingers tapping the table where he distinctly remembered leaving his mobile.

"Clever girl," he muttered under his breath, glancing up as a reflected flicker of movement caught his eye in the highly polished chrome of the cooker hood opposite.

Reacting on pure instinct, Luke grabbed the champagne bottle and in one swiftly fluid movement, turned and hurled it at the man in the doorway, catching him by surprise.

The gun in his hand jerked upwards and fired, dislodging a chunk of plaster from the ceiling as Luke threw himself bodily onto him, knocking the gun flying from his hand and sending the would-be assassin crashing to the ground.

Grabbing a long, wicked shard of broken glass, Luke dropped onto the man's chest and held it to his throat.

"Where is he?" he demanded. The man choked with fear, eyes bulging as Luke pressed the lethally sharp edge into his skin.

"Where's he taken her?" he yelled, seeing sweat break out on the other man's face.

"Airfield somewhere," the man gasped.

"Which airfield?"

"I don't know!" He yelped with fear as Luke increased the pressure. "Honestly, I don't," he screamed. "He never told me. I wasn't going with them, so I didn't need to know. All I know is he wanted his wife, and he sent a couple of men to get the kid, that's all I know, I swear."

Stifling a curse, recognising the ring of truth in the terrified man's voice, Luke slammed his head on the floor, feeling a twinge of satisfaction as the man's eyes rolled up into his head and he passed out.

"Blackwood? Blackwood!"

Becoming aware of William's voice yelling at him from the phone lying on the kitchen floor, Luke picked it up.

"I'm okay," he said, feeling his side and relieved his stitches appeared to have held. Glancing up at the shiny cooker hood, he mentally made a note to give his cleaner a rise.

"We were right, they will be going after Lucia. Get an armed response unit over there. I'll phone Isabella and warn her."

"What about Arianna?" asked Williams.

"She managed to take my mobile."

"Clever girl." Williams echoed Luke's earlier sentiment. "I'll get them tracking it. If it's switched on and she's managed to keep it concealed, we'll find them."

Huddled in the corner of the car, Arianna braced herself as the driver threw the vehicle round a sharp corner, her head connecting with the window.

"Steady on, Nash," cautioned Roberto. "We don't want my wife bruised ... yet." He shot Arianna an evil smile.

She saw the smirk on the driver's face and knew she could expect no help from that quarter. Desperately, she looked out of the window, wondering if she could attract anyone's attention, but the windows were tinted, and this was London. As in any big city, people were busy going about their lives. Arianna knew no one would notice; no one would care.

Frantically, she wondered about Luke, clinging to the hope he was more than capable of taking care of himself, yet couldn't help the small moan of despair which crept from her lips.

Roberto glanced at her and patted her on the hand. "Don't worry, my love," his voice oozed with fake sympathy. "Soon you'll be reunited with Lucia and then we'll all be together again, a happy family on our way to a new life far away."

"Lucia?" stuttered Arianna, staring at him in horror. "What do you mean?"

"You seriously didn't think I'd leave her behind, did you?" Roberto tutted in exasperation, and Arianna's heart constricted with terror.

"Of course, I want our little girl with us, and I'm hopeful we'll soon provide her with a new brother or sister."

He pulled Arianna across the seat towards him, his tongue wet and invasive as he pressed a kiss onto her unwilling mouth.

Shaking with loathing and disgust, Arianna clawed away from him, desperately wiping a hand across her mouth, her eyes spitting fire.

"You will not touch me!" she promised, shuddering at the look in his eyes.

"Oh, but I will," he assured her. "One way or another, Arianna, you will be a proper wife to me again. Willingly or unwillingly, it's all the same to me, but you will be mine."

Arianna shrank away from him, curling into as small a ball as possible whilst he chuckled and looked out of the window, exclaiming as the car drew to a halt at temporary traffic lights, the loud judder of a pneumatic drill penetrating even the thickly insulated interior of the car.

Huddling into the corner, Arianna felt something hard in her pocket pressing against her thigh. Hope exploded in her brain. Of course, Luke's mobile.

Her mind raced. She remembered watching a crime series a month before where the victim had been tracked by satellite via her mobile. Luke's mobile was switched off. If only she could...

Glancing out of the window, Arianna waited until the drill burst into life again. Undercover of its ear-splitting decibels she slipped her hand into her pocket and felt along the phone for the on button, hoping its welcoming jingle would be obliterated by the construction noise outside.

She pressed the button and glanced at Roberto. He was still watching impatiently out of the window, seemingly oblivious to anything she was doing.

Relieved, Arianna withdrew her hand from her pocket, letting it rest in her lap as the lights changed and the car sped forward.

Then, she leaned her head back against the seat, closed her eyes and prayed as she had never prayed before.

~Chapter Twenty-Three~
"It's time to finish this,"

Isabella!"

"Yes?" Isabella frowned at the tightly controlled fear in Luke's voice.

Instinctively, she glanced out of the kitchen window into the garden where Lucia lay happily sprawled on a picnic rug, belly down, bare feet dangling in mid-air, reading a book.

"Santorini's escaped. He's taken Arianna."

"What? How did he ... never mind."

Isabella wiped the shock from her mind and focused to achieve clarity.

"What's the plan?" she asked crisply.

"Arianna managed to take my mobile with her. It's been switched on, so the police are monitoring and following the signal. I'm on my way to rendezvous with them now. The thing is ... Isabella, we know they will be coming after Lucia."

"Yes," she agreed.

"An armed response unit is on its way, but you need to get out of there. Santorini's men could be there at any moment."

"Don't worry," Isabella reassured him, and he heard the steel in her voice. "No one will get anywhere near her."

"Don't try any heroics, Isabella, just get out of there. You don't know what you'll be up against. His men will be armed and ruthless. Don't try to take them on alone, you could get hurt."

"All right," Isabella agreed meekly.

Luke frowned at her easy capitulation.

"I mean it, Isabella," he warned. "I have to go; I'll call your mobile and let you know what's happening. You get Lucia out of there as quickly as possible. Those men mean business."

"So, do I, Luke," Isabella murmured as she put the phone down. "So, do I."

Lucia looked up when her aunt came back into the garden carrying a tall glass of dark, fizzy cola, usually a banned substance. Her eyes gleamed with pleasure as Isabella smiled and held the glass out to her.

"Coke, wow, thanks, Auntie Bella."

She gratefully took the drink and gulped happily at it.

Her aunt settled on the blanket beside her and watched her niece drink, the smile on her face not reaching her eyes as Lucia's eyelids began to droop, and the glass slipped from her hand onto the grass.

"That's right," she murmured, lifting the unconscious child into her arms, and carrying her carefully back indoors.

"You sleep, my darling. It will make this so much easier."

The house looked still, empty even, yet the man watching it knew the occupants had not left. As the two men in black, with blank, hooded eyes and unsmiling mouths crossed the road to his vantage point, he gestured impatiently.

"Took your bloody time, didn't you?" he grumbled. The men merely looked at him, their expressions forcing a shiver of fear down his spine.

"Are they in there?" one of them snapped.

"Yeah," the private eye nodded. "The woman and the kid, they're in there. I haven't seen the kid since they went in, but the woman looked out the front window a few minutes ago."

"The woman is unimportant," interrupted the second man in black. "Only the child matters."

"So, what are you going to do with them?" he asked uneasily, not at all sure he wanted to know.

"That is not your concern." They studied him dispassionately, the chill down his spine turning to icy cold fear at the underlying menace in their eyes.

"Right," he mumbled, suddenly wishing to be as far away from them as possible. "I'll be off then. I'll send the invoice to the usual place, shall I?"

"Yes," they agreed, then seemed to dismiss him, their attention focused on the house and its vulnerable occupants.

He had a sudden memory of the woman and the child as they looked when he saw them going into the house, loaded down with shopping bags, laughing together. The woman's hand had rested gently on the top of the child's shining, dark head as she fumbled for keys and let them in.

Swallowing down the foolhardy, although brave protest which welled up in his throat, he instead turned and walked away, feeling small and cowardly for simply abandoning them to their fate. Knowing the two in black wouldn't hesitate to kill him should he even think of lifting a finger to help the doomed woman and child.

They watched him go.

"Will he be trouble?" one asked.

The other shook his head. "No." His lip curled in disdain. "He's too worried about his own skin to cause any trouble."

Noiselessly, they slipped down the alleyway which ran along the back of the houses, easily locating the garden belonging to their target. Silently, they lifted the latch on the gate and entered the sunny, sheltered patch, empty except for a plaid picnic rug and the discarded remains of lunch.

The back door stood open. From inside the house floated the sound of a popular song coming from upstairs. Easing their way into the kitchen, they both drew their weapons.

"Lucia!"

Halfway down the hall, they froze, as the woman's voice, tinged with annoyance, came from the room located to the right.

"Turn it down a bit, honey, I'm trying to watch the news."

There was no reply from upstairs, although the music did decrease in volume slightly. The lead man gestured upwards, the other nodded, silently slipping down the hall. Soundlessly, he began to mount the stairs.

Slowly, the other eased open the door which stood ajar, realising it led to a lounge. Bright images of a 24-hour news channel flickered on a plasma screen in the corner.

He paused, eyes sweeping the room for its occupant, and saw the glossy, dark cap of her hair visible over the top of a large, chocolate leather armchair positioned in front of the TV.

He moved into the room, his inaudible progress telling of a lifetime of practice.

Closer and closer he moved. Reaching the chair, he pressed the gun against the back of her head, glancing down as he eased back the trigger, eyes bulging with shock as he saw ... no one.

A dark wig on a ball mounted on the end of a long stick, that was in turn wedged into the sofa cushions, artfully created the impression of someone sitting in the chair.

Startled and concerned, he turned, and had a snapshot impression of cropped, black hair and glittering, dark eyes, before a savage chop from a hand that felt like iron lashed the gun from his hand, sweeping upward to deliver a debilitating blow to the side of his throat.

He fell, his last conscious thought being how much she looked like her brother.

Isabella oozed silently up the stairs.

The man she was following was good, but she was better, her sharp ears and heightened senses aware of his progress as he moved from room to room, seeking Lucia.

He stopped in the bathroom, scanning the small space with something akin to panic. He'd checked every room. There was no sign of anyone, just music playing from a speaker in the master bedroom.

Frowning, he turned to re-check the rooms and was knocked viciously backwards by a powerful kick which jolted the gun from his hand and sent him crashing into the sink.

Winded and angry, he surged forward with a howl of rage, as he realised not only was his attacker unarmed but was a woman.

He punched, his fist passing through thin air as she ducked, whirled, and kicked a powerful blow to the solar plexus which left him gasping for air.

Realising too late he had underestimated his opponent, he looked for the gun, locating it wedged behind the back of the toilet. Desperately, he dove for it, beefy fingers scrabbling to retrieve it.

"Oh no you don't," she said.

He turned, gun in his fingertips as she leapt onto him, knee coming down painfully onto his wrist, the flat of her hand slamming upwards, crunching his nose in a red veil of pain. She gripped his numb wrist.

With one sharp twist, the gun was in her hand. He saw it rise, it connected heavily with the side of his head, and he knew no more.

Isabella bound them, left them for the police to find, and then hurried out to the garage where the sleeping Lucia barely stirred on the backseat of her car as she jumped in and turned the key. Snatching out her mobile, she punched in a number.

"Anything?" She listened, head to one side, as a location was relayed to her, eyes narrowing with satisfaction as she pressed the remote to open the garage doors.

"It's time to finish this," she muttered, and the car shot forward with a screech of tyres.

~Chapter Twenty-Four~
"I'll take her to hell with me!"

They drove for what felt like hours, despair pulling Arianna further and further down. She watched carefully, hopeful for some clue as to their destination, seeing the hustle of inner London being replaced with the grime and hopelessness of some of the poorer districts.

Now they were speeding through leafy suburbs, out into the countryside.

It started to rain. As Arianna stared at the droplets trickling down the window, she felt they aptly reflected the desolation in her heart.

She worried about Luke and Lucia, praying Luke had survived the attack by the granite-faced man Roberto had sent to kill him; that Isabella and Lucia had gone out shopping or to the cinema; anything rather than staying at home.

Finally, the car turned off the road and passed through a large pair of ornate, metal gates. With a sinking heart, Arianna saw a runway, and a collection of small planes and knew they had reached their destination.

There was no hope left of a rescue now.
No one knew where she was.
No one could reach her in time.
No one was coming for her.

She was alone.

Her breath caught painfully in her chest when she saw the plane standing at the end of the runway with yet another black-clad man leaning against it, obviously waiting for them, his jaw moving over the gum in his mouth.

He straightened when he saw them, seemingly oblivious to the rain splashing onto his bare head.

The car purred to a halt. Another man stepped forward, bending his head as Roberto pressed a button and his window slid smoothly down.

"Is my child here yet?" he demanded.

"Not yet, Mr Santorini," he replied.

Roberto's face darkened.

"They should have been here by now," he snapped. "What about Blackwood?"

"Bates hasn't reported in," the other man said, swallowing nervously at the obvious fury on his employer's face. "I'll phone them," he added hastily.

Roberto curtly nodded, his window sliding up over the man's spluttering apologies.

"We'll wait here a few moments for Lucia," Roberto declared.

Arianna shrank back as he suddenly gripped her hand and pressed a firm kiss to her palm, his eyes glittering up at her.

"Not long to wait now," he declared. "I have missed my family. It will be good to have you near me again."

"If you missed us that much," Arianna gasped, dragging her hand away from his grasp, "why did you wait so long? Six years, Roberto? Lucia didn't even know you were still alive."

"Ah, yes," his eyes darkened with anger. "I must admit to being surprised my child knew nothing about me."

"What was I supposed to tell her? That you were a thief? That the police were after you? They're not exactly qualities that make a good father. I hoped to never see you again. It seemed kinder if Lucia didn't know the truth about you."

"I did it for us," stated Roberto. "So that we could have an amazing life together."

"For us?" exclaimed Arianna, scornfully. "At least admit the truth to me, Roberto. You did it for yourself. You wanted the money, that's all you've ever been interested in, money!"

"That's not entirely true, my dear," he retorted, gripping her jaw in his thin, strong fingers, and forcing her face towards him.

"I was very interested in you, Arianna. From the moment my father first spoke of you, of your youth, beauty, and breeding, I knew you would be mine no matter what."

"You never loved me though," snarled Arianna, wrenching herself free of his grasp, her mind desperately flying to thoughts of Luke; of his humour and tenderness with her. Her heart ached at the thought of never seeing him again.

"You don't know what it is to love," she cried, rubbing at her sore jaw.

"Oh, and I suppose Blackwood does?" Roberto's voice was silky smooth, yet Arianna could hear the madness beneath the words.

"Yes," she declared bravely, lifting her chin in defiance. "Luke knows what it is to truly love another more than you love yourself, something you'll never know Roberto. So, you might as well let me go because I'll always hate you and I'll never stop loving him."

"Enough!" snapped Roberto and flung open the car door. "What's happening?" he cried, as the man hurried forward, clutching a phone in shaking hands, his face ashen with unwelcome news.

"I couldn't get answers from any of their phones," he said, compulsively swallowing, his eyes darting nervously to meet Roberto's then sliding away as if to hide from him.

"So, I called Samuels. He told me Blackwood's still alive, and the men you sent to get the child are in custody."

"What?" Roberto howled in disbelief.

Arianna's heart soared. They were safe, Luke and Lucia were safe.

"Then we won't wait another minute," declared Roberto. He dragged Arianna out of the car by her arm.

"It looks like it's just you and me, wife," he drawled, and Arianna struggled against his grip.

"I won't go with you!" she screamed, gasping when Roberto pulled her close to him, arms enfolding her tightly, breath hot on the back of her neck.

"You will go wherever I decide you go," he murmured, running his hand down her body, feeling her naked form through the thin, cotton dress.

"I haven't forgotten what it was like to make love to you," he whispered.

Arianna strained away, disgust rising in her throat as his touch slithered over her hips.

"I'm looking forward to making you scream with pleasure beneath me," he continued. "In fact, there's a bed on the plane. Why waste any more time, when I could be enjoying my wife, hearing her moan my name and beg for more..."

"Never!" Arianna cried, and his low answering chuckle raised the hairs on the back of her neck as she struggled and twisted in his grasp.

"Oh, you'll beg, Arianna, I promise you, you'll beg ... What's this?"

His fingers stopped as they encountered the bulge of the phone in her pocket.

Roughly, he reached in and pulled it out, his eyes widening as he saw what it was, realising what it meant.

"Everyone in the plane!" he yelled, crushing the phone underfoot. "We're going now."

Quickly, men began rushing towards the plane. Roberto seized a handful of Arianna's hair, twisting her head around cruelly to face him.

"I suppose you think you're very clever, don't you?" he murmured.

Arianna fought to keep the fear from her face. "Only compared to you," she replied and had the satisfaction of seeing his face darken with anger. His hand raised as if to strike her.

Bravely, Arianna lifted her chin, her eyes never leaving his, daring him to.

Suddenly, they heard sirens.

Panic flashed over his face, his hand dropped to his side, and he began to pull her roughly towards the plane.

Resisting, her bare feet scraping over course tarmac, the raindrops stinging her face, Arianna cried out with pain as he cruelly twisted her arm, dragging her inch by reluctant inch towards the plane.

Arianna knew if he got her on board, if they flew away, the chances of Luke finding her were remote. They got lucky before when Roberto took Lucia. The odds of being so fortunate again were impossible.

"Arianna!"

At Luke's cry, Arianna's head snapped round to see police cars pouring onto the airfield, encircling the runway. Armed police leapt from cars, taking up positions, and there, jumping from the lead car was Luke, closely followed by a tall, heavily built man, whose power and authority were obvious even from where she was standing.

"It's over, Santorini," Williams declared. "You're surrounded. Put down your weapons and come peacefully."

Arianna glanced at Roberto's men, saw indecision and panic on their faces, and knew the situation could quickly degenerate into a shoot-out. She tried to move away from Roberto, but he yanked her tighter, his gun cold against her throat.

"Let her go, Santorini!" ordered Luke.

"And lose my only bargaining chip!"

"Take one more step towards that plane and you'll be shot where you stand," threatened Williams.

"Then I'll take her to hell with me!"

Arianna heard the sneer in Roberto's voice as he moved her body to shield his, the gun pressing with increasing force against her neck.

Luke's heart missed a beat with fear as he saw in the other man's eyes how serious that threat was.

Desperately, he looked at Arianna. Her eyes locked intently onto his, her expression one of mingled relief at seeing him alive and unharmed, and fear at what might happen next.

As he watched, a strangely determined look crossed her face. He wondered what she was thinking.

Arianna was angry with herself, annoyed she hadn't paid more attention when Isabella had tried to teach her self-defence. But they'd had a bottle of wine and the session had quickly degenerated into a farce, with the girls collapsing, breathless and giggling, onto the sofa.

Now, Arianna cursed her stupidity for not learning anything, for not even trying. All she could remember was Isabella saying once you made up your mind to attack you must carry it through with everything you've got and mean it. That was the key, to intend to hurt your opponent.

Most women can't bring themselves to you see, Isabella had stated, eyes narrowing as she tried to show Arianna the pressure points of the body. It's not in a woman's nature to hurt, she continued, they must be provoked.

Luke took a step forward. Arianna felt the shock of the gun slamming up into her jaw.

"You want to kill her, you just keep on coming," warned Roberto, and Luke stepped back.

Arianna's body went limp as she appeared to faint, sagging heavily into Roberto's arms. He staggered back, shoved off-balance, trying to steady himself as he took her unexpected weight.

Instantly, Arianna exploded upwards, the top of her head connecting violently with the underneath of Roberto's jaw, at the same time as one arm jerked upwards knocking his gun arm away.

She spun around, rabbit punched him in the throat, before turning on her heel and running as fast as she could towards Luke.

In slow motion, Luke saw Santorini drop to his knees, saw him recover and raise his gun.

"Arianna!" yelled Luke, pulling his gun, desperately trying to get a fix on Santorini.

But she was in the way, dark hair flying, eyes terrified. She ran, her back an easy target. Luke sprang forward, his powerful legs closing the distance between them as he raced towards her.

Santorini's men were also raising their weapons. Behind him, Luke heard William's roar.

"Hold your fire, you might hit the woman!"

There was a sharp crack of a gun, followed instantly by another.

~Chapter Twenty-Five~
"Please, look after Lucia for me..."

Luke saw the shock on her face.
Knew she'd been hit.
Her body jerked violently forward.
Her arms flew wide.
Her head snapped back with the force, and she began to fall.

A howl of anguish was ripped from Luke's throat as he reached her, caught her as she fell, cradling her in his arms.

Blood, so much blood, oh dear god, there was so much blood.

Tenderly, he wiped the hair from her eyes, the rain from her face, and heard the pounding of feet as Williams reached him.

"Get an ambulance here immediately," he ordered, and an officer rushed to do his bidding

Luke's heart broke as she opened her beautiful, green eyes, and stared at him in dazed incomprehension, her hand groping for his, her breath rasping out in pain-filled gasps.

"Lucia?" she begged.

"She's okay," he assured her. "She's with Isabella. We got the men Santorini sent for her."

Satisfied, Arianna nodded, looking deep into his eyes.

"I love you," she murmured.

Luke bent over, trying to protect her from the lashing rain with his body, his large hand cupping her face as she pulled him to her, and he kissed her cold, cold lips.

"Roberto?" she asked.

Luke looked at Williams who was crouched beside the prone body of Santorini. Slowly, he rose to his feet, turned, and shook his head at Luke.

He stepped aside and Luke saw the frozen grimace on Santorini's face, the stunned shock in his staring eyes, the neat hole to the side of his head, and the spreading puddle of blood.

"He's dead," he told her bluntly.

His body clutched with fear as her eyes glazed over, and he sensed her slipping away into a shadowy world where he couldn't follow.

"Arianna!"

Panic made his voice rough.

Her eyes opened and she smiled wearily.

"So tired," she murmured. "I need to sleep for a little while."

"No, you can't," he insisted. "You're going into shock. You must stay awake, Arianna. Stay with me, please, please stay with me!"

"Luke…"

His name left her lips on a sigh.

Blood was pooling beneath her now, diluting and spreading, her life force being washed away in the rain.

Clutching her to him, Luke was dimly aware of Williams stripping off his overcoat and shoving it roughly beneath her, trying to stem the flow.

Frantically Luke shook her.

"Don't you dare leave me!" he ordered.

Arianna gasped a low, breathy laugh.

"So bossy," she muttered. He heard the love in her voice as her eyelids fluttered down.

"Arianna Santorini, I love you." Luke's voice was intense with pain.

"Will you marry me?"

"W-what?" Her eyes snapped open.

With relief, he saw the lucidity flood back into them.

"What did you say?"

"I said, will you marry me?"

A beautiful smile spread across her face.

"Oh yes, yes please," she answered.

Gently, he wiped at the tears spilling from her eyes, which mingled with the rain on her cheeks.

"You have to stay awake now," he demanded, fear that he was losing her hoarsening his voice.

"Start planning the wedding," he commanded. "It can be whenever, whatever and wherever you please. Think about your dress, Lucia's dress, the flowers, the rings … everything."

Seeing her eyelids droop, Luke gently shook her by the shoulders."

"There's so much to plan and think about. Arianna, you've got to stay awake."

"Oh," her mouth formed a circle of pleasure.

Luke heard the distant sound of another siren and knew that help was almost there.

"Hold on, Arianna," he begged. "Hold on a little bit longer, please…"

Desperately, he tried to protect her from the lashing rain with his body, tried to anchor her, to keep her here, with him.

"I'm sorry," she whispered. "So sorry. Please, look after Lucia for me…"

Her beautiful eyes stilled and closed.

What was it with hospital coffee? Luke looked with distaste at the sludge at the bottom of the plastic cup.

Would it be so difficult to at least attempt to make it taste like coffee? But then it *was* his sixth cup, each sip tainted with the sharp flavour of concern.

Arianna had been in surgery for hours, and although the surgeons had been hopeful, Luke still paced, fretted, worried, and drank endless cups of disgusting coffee.

"Luke, sit down," Isabella ordered. "You're making us all nervous."

Sheepishly, Luke looked around the waiting room and saw the understanding on the surrounding faces, grateful to his family who came running the moment they heard.

Sitting next to Isabella who was cuddling a scared Lucia, was Susannah.

The two women had been conversing in low, concerned voices, and Luke sensed a bond forming between them.

On the other side of Lucia, already delighted with her future granddaughter, was his mother. Her subtle perfume and richly patterned silk scarf were a welcome relief in the drabness of the waiting room.

Marcus was there, his handsome face set and solemn in its concern.

Next to him sat Kristina, Luke's youngest half-sister.

Luke was touched that even though Arianna and Lucia were strangers to Kit because they were important to Luke, she was here for him, giving her silent support and love.

Finally, there was Siobhan, Liam and Kit's mother, his father's last and youngest wife.

As Luke looked at the kind, lovely face of his young stepmother, he felt a fierce stab of love and pride for his eccentric and extraordinary family.

There was a movement in the doorway.

As one they all looked up to see the surgeon standing there, her white coat and quietly confident manner instantly instilling trust and reassurance.

As Luke stepped forward with Isabella though, he saw the dark shadows and the exhaustion in her eyes.

"Ms Santorini?"

"Yes?" said Isabella quickly.

"How is she?" asked Luke.

"I'm sorry," the doctor glanced at him. "You are...?"

"Her fiancé," Isabella finished for him.

The doctor nodded and glanced around the crowded waiting room, her face softening as she saw Lucia, her eyes wide and scared, fixed on the doctor's face, waiting for her to speak, as they all were.

"The operation went very well," the doctor stated, and an audible sigh of relief swept through the room.

"We were able to retrieve the bullet," she continued. "And luckily, because of the angle of the entry, it didn't do too much damage inside and no internal organs were hit. She's going to be very sore and will have to take things easy for a while, but she's going to be fine."

The doctor smiled wearily at them.

"As I said, she was very lucky. If the bullet hadn't entered at precisely the angle it did, things could have been a lot worse."

"Can we see her?" Isabella asked.

"She's asking to see her daughter, and you Ms Santorini, and …" the doctor smiled at Luke.

"Are you Luke?" she asked. Luke nodded. "Well," she continued. "She's been asking for you too."

~Chapter Twenty-Six~
"A matching pair,"

The private room in which Arianna lay was quiet and soothing after the noise and bustle of the corridors.

Entering behind the doctor, Luke found himself holding his breath as his eyes flew to the narrow bed and its occupant.

"Mummy," cried Lucia.

She rushed forward, clambering onto the chair beside the bed to lean over her mother, the doctor catching her arm before she could climb up next to her.

"Gently now," she cautioned, so Lucia had to be satisfied with holding Arianna's hand, who smiled at her daughter, gently stroking her hair when Lucia lay her head down on the bed next to her mother's side.

"Lucia," she murmured. "I was so worried …" She glanced up, her eyes seeking and finding Isabella's.

"Thank you," she said. "For looking after her."

"Well of course I did," Isabella replied fiercely, and Luke had the feeling she was fighting back tears.

"You're the only family I've got, although…" She shot Luke a highly amused look. "I understand I'm about to gain more relations than I'll know what to do with."

Arianna smiled weakly.

Isabella took Lucia's hand and gently pulled her away.

"Come on, Lucia," she said. "Let's leave these two lovebirds together while you and I go and check out the chocolate machine."

"Okay," Lucia readily agreed, plainly happy to have reassured herself her mother was alive and well and drawn by the promise of chocolate.

"Goodnight, Mummy," she said.

"Goodnight, darling," Arianna looked lovingly into her eyes.

"Be good for Auntie Bella, and I'll see you again soon."

Isabella and Lucia left the room.

The doctor fussed over Arianna before turning to Luke with a smile.

"Ten minutes," she cautioned. "And then Arianna must try to get some rest."

"Of course," Luke agreed.

The doctor bustled out and they were finally alone together.

Self-consciously, he moved to sit on the chair recently vacated by Lucia and reached for Arianna's hand.

"I don't think I've ever been so scared in all my life," he said. "When I realised that he had taken you … I thought I'd lost you forever."

"I know," she murmured, gently squeezing his hand. "I was terrified too, for Lucia and you. When he sent that man up to kill you, even though I knew you were more than capable of looking after yourself, I was so afraid he'd take you by surprise."

"He nearly did," Luke confessed wryly. "If it hadn't been for a very shiny cooker hood, he would have managed it."

"What?" asked Arianna, confused.

Luke smiled and shook his head. "Never mind."

"And then," Arianna continued, "when I heard you were both okay, that the men who'd gone to fetch Lucia were in custody, oh, the relief!"

"How did you know that?" Luke asked curiously.

Arianna frowned wearily.

"One of Roberto's men. He tried to call the others but couldn't get an answer, so he spoke to someone called Samuels who told him you were still alive, and the men had been arrested."

Luke nodded, filing the name away to pass onto Williams, wondering if this was possibly the source of the leaked information.

"Luke," Arianna's voice was low.

As he looked at her, she flushed, eyes sliding away from his, her other hand plucking nervously at the bedspread.

"Before … what you said, when you…"

She paused and took a deep breath as if forcing herself to go on.

"… asked me to marry you, I understand you were trying to stop me from going into shock and I wanted to say, I don't hold you to it. The situation we were in, well, it was … difficult, and well, what I'm trying to say is, I don't want you to feel obligated in any way, or feel you've been backed into a corner…"

Listening to her stuttering speech, his eyebrows raised with amusement, Luke decided he had heard enough, leant forward, and kissed her, thoroughly and soundly, pouring his heart and soul into the kiss and showing her exactly what she meant to him.

He felt her soft lips part in surprise, then her response, spontaneous and flammable.

Mindful of her condition, Luke pulled back, eyeing her flushed cheeks and glazed expression with satisfaction.

"I asked you to marry me because I can't imagine spending the rest of my life with anyone except you," he stated firmly. "Although," he continued. "I will quite understand if you've changed your mind, after all, it was a difficult situation."

In answer, Arianna yanked him back down to her, and several highly satisfactory minutes passed before he sat back in his chair and smiled smugly.

"So," he began. "I take it we are now officially engaged. Once you're back on your feet we'll need to go shopping for a ring. A big ring. A really, *really* big ring."

"No," she muttered. "Not a big ring, a small, tiny ring."

Her eyes were shining, although the tiredness was obvious.

Glancing at the clock, he saw his ten minutes were almost up.

"We'll discuss it later," he promised. "But I should go now. Let you get some sleep."

"I forgot to ask," Arianna muttered sleepily. "How's your wound?"

"It's fine," he replied, his fingers gingerly feeling his side, smiling as Arianna copied his movement, gently touching her own bandaged torso.

A flicker of amusement crossed her weary expression, as she too noticed their injuries were in almost identical places.

"A matching pair," she murmured.

Gently, he kissed her on the forehead.

"Always," he replied quietly and slipped from the room.

Outside, he found Chief Inspector Williams leaning against the wall waiting for him, his weary, rumpled face concerned and pensive as he sipped distastefully at a cup of hospital issue coffee.

"How is she?" he asked.

Luke smiled thankfully. "She's going to be okay."

Williams nodded thoughtfully, his thickset, untidy body in its crumpled, old-fashioned, brown suit looking strangely at odds in the starkly sterile atmosphere of the hospital.

"She told me something you might find of interest," Luke continued.

Williams' expression darkened with anger as Luke told him about the information Roberto's man had gained from a source known as Samuels.

"I take it that name means something to you?"

"Oh yes," Williams muttered, scrunching up his cup and throwing it angrily into the nearest bin. "It means something all right. Thanks for that, Blackwood."

His mouth snapped shut, and Luke realised no more was to be said on the subject.

"We've got a bit of a mystery on our hands, Blackwood," he continued.

Luke frowned, curiously. "What's that?"

"I've been talking to the officers who had a clear sightline on Santorini at the time of the shooting. They all agree that Santorini had a clear shot at Arianna. She was only feet away from him. There's no way that shouldn't have been a kill shot, no way he could have missed her heart, except..."

"Except?" prompted Luke.

"Except, someone shot him first. He pulled the trigger as he was falling, that's why the bullet missed her back and went through her side. That's why she's in there now with a fighting chance, not lying down in the morgue with a bullet through her heart."

"Well then that someone deserves a medal," declared Luke stoutly.

"I happen to agree with you," Williams shrugged. "But that's where the mystery comes into it. Not one of my officers shot him, and I've just heard from ballistics. The bullet they dug out of him doesn't come from any police-issued weapon."

"What?" Luke stared at him in surprise. "What do you mean?"

"I mean," began Williams slowly. "Whoever shot Santorini, it wasn't one of my men."

"One of his own?" hazarded Luke.

Again, Williams shook his head.

"Bullet doesn't match their guns either," he claimed.

Luke looked baffled.

"So, what you're saying," he began slowly, "is that Roberto Santorini was shot by someone who wasn't there."

"In a nutshell, yeah," drawled Williams. "Like I said, a bit of a mystery..."

Wandering back to the waiting room, Luke turned the information Williams had given him over in his head, looking at it from every angle, trying to understand.

Finally, he gave up and sent a mental blessing to whomever it was who shot Santorini first, stopping him from shooting his wife at point-blank range in the back, and thereby saving her life.

Whoever they were, he owed them everything. One day, he hoped that somehow, he would be able to repay them.

In the doorway of the waiting room, he paused, his heart lifting in gratitude for his noisy, chaotic family who had always been there for him throughout his life.

Now they were here for Arianna and Lucia, welcoming them without reservation into the Blackwood clan.

As if sensing his regard, Isabella lifted her head and stared levely at him.

As he looked back into her dark, fathomless eyes, a sudden, fantastical thought gripped Luke and he wondered.

Then Isabella smiled, turned her attention back to Lucia, and the thought passed, pushed away as being too incredible to be true.

Because if true, it would mean that Isabella ... but it was too farfetched to even consider.

Wasn't it?

Tucking away the thought to be mulled over later and realising that – if it were true – then there was a massive debt to be repaid at some point, Luke smiled at the concerned faces of his family.

"She's going to be fine," he told them, and sat next to his mother, grunting in amusement as Lucia threw herself bodily into his arms for a big bear hug.

"I'm so happy I found you, Daddy," she whispered in his ear, and Luke bent his face into her soft hair to hide the tears welling in his eyes.

He thought he'd lost everything, but now realised he'd found the world.

~One Year Later~
"She has the look of her father,"

She had noticed the family the day before, smiling as she watched them play on the beach and in the sea.

The father, tall, strong, and handsome; the mother, slim, dark, stunningly beautiful; their daughter, a bright firecracker of a child who dashed between her parents, sharing her affection and attention equally between them.

But today, the elderly lady noticed the woman sitting alone at a beachside table, shading her eyes with her hand as she looked out to sea.

Following her gaze, the lady saw the man and child in the water, and she watched as he patiently and skilfully attempted to teach the child how to windsurf.

His rich laugh echoed over the beach as the child fell off into the brilliant, azure blue of the shallow ocean, his arms strong as he lifted her back to her feet, encouraging her not to give in, but to try again, always try again.

Curiously, the lady settled herself at the next beach table. Her companions had all gone for their afternoon naps, but she refused to even countenance the idea.

There was plenty of time for napping when you were dead, she always stated fiercely.

Besides, they only had another three days left in this stunningly gorgeous slice of paradise, and she for one intended to make the most of it.

Discreetly, she glanced at the younger woman, her sharp eyes noticing the classic, plain gold wedding band, and the exquisite, tastefully small emerald engagement ring, plainly visible as she lifted her hand to push a strand of hair from her cheek.

Finally, the old lady could contain herself no longer. Striking up conversations with total strangers had been a lifelong habit of hers.

As her beloved Hubert, may his soul rest in peace, used to say, you could set his Ida on a desert island, and she would attempt to have a chat with a coconut.

"She's doing very well, isn't she?" she ventured.

The younger woman turned smiling eyes to her, pride in her daughter written all over her face.

"Yes, she is," she agreed. Ida heard the accent, English, classy too.

"Considering she could barely swim when we first got here," the young woman continued. "She's done amazingly well."

"How long are you here for?" Ida asked curiously.

"We have another week," the woman confided. "We've already had two, I wish we could stay longer but school will be starting soon, and we need to be home in time for that."

"I'm surprised you're not out there with them," Ida stated, then watched curiously as a warm glow suffused the younger woman's face.

"I wanted to have a go," she replied, "but my husband wouldn't hear of it. He's very ... protective of me right now," she continued.

Her hand rested lightly on her stomach, and she shared a look with the elderly lady.

A look that women had been exchanging since time immemorial; a look which Ida understood immediately.

"Oh, my dear," she exclaimed in delight. "How wonderful! How far along are you?"

"Thirteen weeks," the woman replied, and smiled. "It's been an easy pregnancy so far, but my husband worries about me so."

"Well of course he does," the old woman agreed hotly. "And quite right too."

A companionable silence fell over them as they both looked out to where the girl had managed to clamber onto the child-sized board and was balancing precariously, face alight with the triumph of achievement.

Voice raised in excitement, she cried out to her mother to look at what she was doing. Dutifully, they waved and clapped.

Ida turned kindly eyes to her young companion.

"How lovely," she said. "To have a little brother or sister for your daughter, I always think it's nice, not to be an only."

"Yes," the young woman agreed. "I'm an only, but my husband comes from a large family, and I envy him the closeness of his brothers and sisters."

"She's the dead spit of you," the woman exclaimed, then paused, head on one side as she considered.

"And yet," she continued, "she has the look of her father. The same angle of the chin and that determined expression. Now I look closer, she looks very much like him, don't you think?"

"Yes," the young woman replied firmly, flashing the elderly lady a warm smile. "I think you're right. She does look like him, just like her father."

And Arianna Blackwood smiled happily to herself, settling back in her chair, the Caribbean sun warm on her face as she watched her husband and their daughter play in the water, her hand resting gently on the soft mound of her stomach.

She had lost so much in her life but now had found everything she could ever want or need.

She thought about how happy she was.

She had found the one person she was meant to be with, and life was good.

The End...

If you have enjoyed reading

Lost & Found

Turn the page for a sneak
peek at book two of the
Blackwood Family Saga

Fixtures & Fittings

Where the story continues with
Marcus Blackwood

~Chapter One~
"Just come, Marcus, please, just come..."

Marcus Blackwood had discovered it was entirely possible for him to fall asleep with his eyes open.

So gifted had he become at this skill that he was able to completely convince the person he was talking to that he was awake, lucid, and giving his whole attention to the matter in hand, when in fact, Marcus was drifting away in a land which existed nowhere else but inside his head.

This talent had saved his sanity during many a long meeting, and as the head of acquisitions and mergers regurgitated an incomprehensible wedge of facts, figures, and forecasts in a monotonous and, dare Marcus even think it, downright boring voice, he could feel his grip on reality beginning to slip.

Sitting bolt upright in his incredibly uncomfortable chair, Marcus blinked several times in a desperate attempt to focus on what was probably very important information.

However, his thoughts were reluctant to obey. Sulky and truculent, they whined and complained about being forced to waste their precious time on such rubbish.

Pay attention, Marcus ordered himself. It was no good. With all the wild enthusiasm of boisterous puppies, his thoughts slipped from his grasp and frisked away into the distance, eager to explore and see what was over the hill.

It didn't help that it was a hot and sticky day. The golden eye of the late afternoon sun streaming through shut windows boiling its occupants, as sluggish air conditioning fought to deal with such an unusually warm British May.

Was it any wonder Marcus's imaginings longed to be anywhere but here? Longed to be somewhere cool and shady where he could relax, loosen his tie, and slip off his tight, patent leather shoes in which his toes squirmed in sweaty, cramped misery.

"Don't you agree, Marcus?"

Marcus blinked, instantly back in the room, realising for once his skill had let him down. He paused, hoping inspiration would strike, unwilling to let his colleagues know he wasn't listening. That all their carefully prepared reports and flow charts had been for nothing because the boss had been asleep.

Eight pairs of expectant slightly sycophantic eyes gazed at him.

A sheen of panic glazed his forehead and Marcus knew he had to say something. He had a fifty-fifty chance of getting it right and hell, even if he got it wrong no one was going to argue with the boss.

'That's a complex question, Nigel," he stalled, and Nigel nodded seriously, myopic gaze blinking behind thick lenses.

"And one that needs a good deal of consideration." Marcus prayed Nigel hadn't asked if it was time to stop for coffee.

His intercom buzzed.

Thankfully, he lunged at it, deciding even though he'd told his PA not to allow any calls through, she deserved a raise.

"Yes?"

"Marcus, you have a call on line one."

Sally's voice was low with concern. Marcus frowned at the taut worry he heard in her tone.

"I did say no calls, Sally," he chided, mildly.

"I know, but I think you need to take this one. Marcus, it's your mother…"

"My mother?"

Marcus shifted in surprise, intensely aware of eight pairs of eyes all busily pretending not to be eavesdropping.

"Yes, your mother," continued Sally. "Something's happened, Marcus, and I think you should talk to her alone."

Marcus's brows flew up in surprise.

Sally had been his PA for many years and was fully aware of his feelings concerning his mother. He knew she'd never normally interrupt a meeting with one of his mother's self-imposed crisis calls.

If Sally said it was important; it was important.

"Right," he said slowly. "Put it through to my office and tell her to hang on, I'll take it there. Oh, and Sally, perhaps you could organise some coffee for everyone?"

"Of course, Marcus."

Marcus hung up and looked around the desk.

"If we could have a ten-minute break, I'll take this call and then we can resume."

There was a general round of agreement. A feeling of relaxation descended over the table as people visibly stood down.

Pushing back chairs and stretching, they looked with anticipation towards the door. It was well known that Marcus's PA supplied the best coffee, and sometimes even brought in homemade cookies.

Closing his office door firmly behind him, Marcus took a second to settle into his leather chair, closing his eyes briefly and letting out a sigh as he prepared to deal with his mother.

It wasn't that he didn't love her. Of course, he did, she was his mother. It was more that he didn't understand her.

Maybe it was the fact she was so very American that sometimes made Marcus feel they came from different planets.

Marcus was British, that was how he viewed himself. Despite his mother being American, despite having a dual nationality passport, as far as Marcus was concerned, he was British as his father had been, British through and through.

His parents had enjoyed a surprisingly happy marriage, but his mother hated Britain and his father couldn't stand America.

When they finally decided to amicably separate, their solution had been to split the family neatly down the middle.

Marcus remained in Britain with his father, attending a good public school where he made the necessary connections to enable him to work his way up the ranks in the family business, before taking over following his father's death.

During the holidays he visited his mother and older sister in America, except at Christmas when they all came back to Britain. Then his mother would throw herself into the festivities, declaring it was so good to be back with her family and this time they would stay.

But by the first week in January, she was itching to return to her friends and her charity work, to the throbbing, bustling metropolis of New York, his mother's natural habitat.

Like a fish out of water, Marcus could see her visibly gasping to breathe its polluted air again. He had accepted early on that this was the way they did things in his family.

Living with his father and his second wife, Marina, Marcus had been delighted to have a new brother and sister to keep him company, the three half-siblings forming a bond as close as any full-blooded family.

His half-brother, Luke, being only four years younger than himself, became Marcus's special confidante. Given the continued absence of his older sister Monica and how like his mother she was, Marcus was closer to Luke than her.

Thinking now of his father, Marcus sighed again, unwilling to admit how much he missed him. Since his death, Marcus had been the one to deal with his mother's habitual phone calls about everything and nothing.

Assuming the mantle of arbitrator and advisor, his mother instead called on him to seek his opinion on every minute detail of her, in Marcus's opinion anyway, shallow existence. Bracing himself, he picked up the phone.

"Mother?"

"Marcus, oh thank god, Marcus, the most terrible thing has happened..."

"Calm down, Mother, take a deep breath and tell me what's wrong."

"Oh, Marcus!"

His mother's sobs echoed down the line with chilling clarity.

Marcus straightened in his chair. This wasn't his mother's normal, fluttering panic, this was genuine. This was real.

Sally was right, something was wrong.

Ten minutes later Marcus slowly replaced the handset and slumped at his desk, fingers to his temples, for once in his life unable to deal with the enormity of the situation.

Leaning back, he wiped his eyes, shocked to discover them damp. Fumbling a handkerchief out of his pocket with trembling hands, he dabbed at a face suddenly clammy with shock.

As if she'd been waiting for the line busy light to blink off, Sally slipped into the room bearing a cup of fragrantly steaming coffee which she placed before him. Gratefully, he sipped at it, the reviving liquid easing the knot in his throat.

Glancing at his PA, he noticed that same sunlight beaming onto her shining cap of auburn hair and thought how pretty she was, then the notion was trampled by a fresh wave of despair.

"Sally," he began, stopped, cleared his throat.

"I've dismissed the meeting," she swiftly interrupted. "I told them an emergency had arisen which required you to go to New York and that they were to work on what had been discussed so far, and another meeting will be re-scheduled on your return." Briefly, she glanced at the notepad that she was never without.

"I've managed to get you a one-way ticket to New York on this evening's flight out of Heathrow at 19:09 hours, and I've alerted the car to collect you from here in an hour."

Swallowing the last gulp of coffee Marcus frowned, her calm efficiency allowing his frenzied thoughts to stop, slow down, and assess.

"An hour?" he enquired. "That's not enough time, I need to go home and pack…"

"No need," retorted Sally. Crossing the office, she opened one of the tall, built-in cupboards and removed an overnight case.

"After that time, you needed to leave for the New York office immediately and had to buy all new clothes and toiletries there, I took the liberty of ensuring a bag of essentials was always here, ready and waiting." She paused, reached into the cupboard again and drew out a suit bag.

"There's also a change of suit for you."

Stunned into silent admiration at her forethought, he finally murmured. "But how…?"

"I liaised with your cleaner and she let me in one day. I packed what I thought was necessary and it's been waiting here ever since."

"Sally, never leave me, I don't know what I'd do without you."

A pleased smile flirted with her copper-painted lips. "I'm just doing my job," she murmured.

The flight was packed. Slumped into a window seat, Marcus turned his face away from the other passengers, going over his mother's phone call again and again, and the horror in her voice.

"Something terrible has happened, oh Marcus, something so terrible…"

"Mother, what is it? What's happened?"

"They weren't supposed to be with him, it was a business trip to see a client upstate…"

"Who was?"

"Walter."

Walter was his sister Monica's stuffed shirt of a husband. Marcus had nothing against him, the man was kind and mild-mannered and adored his wife and child, Marcus just found him incredibly dull.

"What about Walter? Mother, you're not making any sense."

"He was going to see a client, it was late, the police aren't sure, but they think it was a carjacking that went wrong, maybe Walter fought back…"

Marcus frowned, finding that thought unlikely, then focused on his mother's words.

"A carjacking? Mother, what…?"

"He's dead, oh Marcus, he's dead!"

The shock jolted him upright. Walter dead? Okay, he hadn't been Marcus's favourite person, but he'd been nice enough. Furthermore, he was family, his sister's husband…

His brain backtracked to her previous statement. "You said, they shouldn't have been with him … Who, Mother? Who was with him?"

"Your sister and Megan were in the car with him. They shouldn't have been, he should have been alone, but at the last minute, Monica decided they needed some family time, so she booked them into a B&B close to his client … they were going for the weekend. It was going to be a special time for them, and now … now…"

"Are they all right? Mother! Are they all right?"

Renewed weeping echoed down the phone, and Marcus's insides turned liquid with horror.

"Just come, Marcus, please, just come…"

Fixtures & Fittings

Amazon

eBook – Paperback –
Free to read on Kindle Unlimited

~About the Author~

Julia Blake lives in the beautiful historical town of Bury St. Edmunds, deep in the heart of the county of Suffolk in the UK, with her daughter, one crazy cat, and a succession of even crazier lodgers.

Her first novel, The Book of Eve, met with worldwide critical acclaim, and since then, Julia has released many other books which have delighted her growing number of readers with their strong plots and instantly relatable characters. Details of all Julia's novels can be found on the next page.

Julia leads a busy life, juggling working and family commitments with her writing, and has a strong internet presence, loving the close-knit and supportive community of fellow authors she has found on social media and promises there are plenty more books in the pipeline.

Julia says: "I write the kind of books I like to read myself, warm and engaging novels, with strong, three-dimensional characters you can connect with."

~ *A Note from Julia* ~

If you have enjoyed this book, why not take a few moments to leave a review on Amazon,

It needn't be much, just a few lines saying you liked the book and why, yet it can make a world of difference.

Reviews are the reader's way of letting the author know they enjoyed their book, and of letting other readers know the book is an enjoyable read and why. It also informs Amazon that this is a book worth promoting, and the more reviews a book receives, the more Amazon will recommend it to other readers.

I would be very grateful and would like to say thank you for reading my book and if you do spare a few minutes of your time to review it, I do see, read, and appreciate every single review left for me.

Best Regards
Julia Blake

~ *Other Books by the Author* ~

The Blackwood Family Saga

Fast-paced and heart-warming, this exciting series tells the story of the Blackwood Family and their search for love and happiness

The Perennials Series

Becoming Lili – the beautiful, coming of age saga
Chaining Daisy – its gripping sequel
Rambling Rose – the triumphant conclusion

The Book of Eve

A story of love, betrayal, and bitter secrets that threaten to rip a young woman's life apart

Black Ice

An exciting steampunk retelling of the Snow White fairy tale

The Forest ~ a tale of old magic ~

Myth, folklore, and magic combine in this engrossing tale of a forgotten village and an ancient curse

Erinsmore

A wonderful tale of an enchanted land of sword and sorcery, myth and magic, dragons, and prophecy

Eclairs for Tea and Other Stories

A fun collection of short stories and quirky poems that reflect the author's multi-genre versatility

Printed in Great Britain
by Amazon